delirium fades

Michael J. Atwood

delirium
fades

This is a work of fiction. All names and events are the product of the author's imagination. Any resemblance to actual people or events is totally coincidental.

No part of this book may be reproduced, scanned or distributed in any printed or electronic form without permission.

Cover Design: Cassy Roop, Pink Ink Designs
Editing & Formatting: Elaine York, Allusion Publishing
www.allusionpublishing.com

Praise for *HiStory of Santa Monica I & II*

Fantastic storytelling. Original characters striving to stay afloat in the very deep and turbulent waters of the Westside of L.A.. Atwood writes like a true roots rocker!

—George Wendt, "Norm" from Cheers, author of *Drinking with George: A Barstool Professional's Guide to Beer*

What these stories make clear is that Atwood's own journey, which fueled this collection has be emphatically worthwhile. Atwood's evocative stories are filled with characters dislocated by their ambitions.

—Dan McGinn, executive editor *Harvard Business Review* and *author of House of Lust: America's Obsession with Our Homes*

What you'll find in the following pages is a portrait to some degree of bridges. The bridges that connect the past to the present, the bridges that connect dreamers, killers, and saints, and the bridges that connect the truth to the lies we tell our selects to pray to God the world believes. In this regard, Atwood's writing ultimately reminds us that in the matter of bridges, it can either be a nail or a match.

—Anthony Cipriano, Creator of The Bates Motel

Available on Amazon or from the author direct with an autograph and personal note.
E-mail atwoodmichaelj@icloud.com

Early Praise for *Delirium Fades*

A delicately woven collection of stories that shines a light on the underbelly of humanity, and in the process, illuminates its soul. Atwood's genius is his ability to take a menagerie of often times unseemly characters and make them heroic. Never mind the paths they walk may lead to the gates of hell.

—Anthony S. Cipriano, Creator of *The Bates Motel* and screenwriter, *Twelve and Holding*

Michael J. Atwood's stories have always delved into the inner lives of real people with the immediacy of a gripping storyteller. Other writers might follow the trends of telling tales of aliens and superheroes. But his characters continue to shed light on the fact that we all might be alien to ourselves and others at times, however tiny heroics are in each of us even with all of our human faults in life.

—Eric Wasserman, author *Celluloid Strangers*

Like being Bourne under a very bad neon sign, characters in 'Delirium Fades' only see flickering chances at redemption. Tales of double-crossed Catholicism and incessant violence populate this taut-as-a-tripwire collection. Despite your better judgment you may find yourself rooting for Omar and Jake aka The Pineapple Kid who lives in a motel. Unforgiving and unforgettable, the delirium tends to linger more than it fades.

—Susan Compo, author of *Warren Oates: A Wild Life* (Screen Classics), *Earthbound: David Bowie and The Man Who Fell To Earth*, and *Pretty Things*

Table of Contents

He remembered well her eyes,
the touch of her hand and his delirium....
But delirium passes.

James Joyce – *Dubliners*

Doubtless, despite his suffering,
he had fallen asleep while walking,
for now he sees another scene—
perhaps he has merely recovered from a delirium.

Ambrose Bierce – "Occurrence at Own Creek Bridge"

AWOL

When the elevator doors opened, Fatalier noticed her immediately. She was among the others in the lobby. He felt his red silk tie tighten around his neck, as his jugular bulged upon her apparition. He was a tall man, in an expensive dark pin-striped suit—an important man. He studied the scene. It was the usual crowd—men, smoking cigarettes, with newspapers tucked underneath their arms, men from the bank. They created patterns of black, blue, and gray with their tailored English suits. He knew they were waiting for girls, most likely secretaries, who ended their day just after 5 PM. He had been there once: he had liked the younger secretaries the best, especially the ones who were less educated. Fatalier turned his eyes back toward her. She had moved, positioning herself among the men as if she was using the crowd to hide. He noticed a zealous, fanatical bitterness in her eyes—delirium. For a moment, Fatalier felt as if he was trapped in a bad dream. He realized that it was him she had come for—this was no coincidental rendezvous. He took a deep breath and reassured himself that they had no relevant business with each other now—too many years had passed. There was no need for any conversation between them. He moved through the lobby, quickly, pushing through the crowd, then out onto the street. He felt that sick sense of perplexity one experiences when caught in a lie by a trusted friend. He had been found.

The afternoon Boston traffic was heavy in the Financial District, and aggravated drivers and cabbies shouted and honked at each other as it began to rain. The chaos reminded Fatalier of the war. He left the curb and walked between the automobiles to create some space if she dared to follow him. The phrase "statute of limitations" ran through his head as he walked briskly. It had been fifteen years since their last encounter—it was 1960 now. Fatalier had investigated the legal consequences of the matter, and, if he was ever caught, jail time would be a certainty, but also the maximum penalty. If he used his wealth to pay a powerful attorney, the explosion that occurred could serve as an excuse: psychological trauma would be their angle.

However, there would be other consequences. There would be the loss of his lucrative position as vice president at the bank, his affluent lifestyle and perhaps even his family. Public humiliation, moral, ethical, and legal embarrassment tended to infect the children and would most assuredly implode a marriage. He had seen it happen before. The children would have to leave their private schools, and the family would have to resign from their private clubs in shame. There were substantial considerations at stake. However, to his relief, it became clear that, if he was caught, there would be no execution—that had not happened since the Civil War. It was instead his unmasking to society that he was concerned about—these matters were guaranteed to show up in the papers. Often, when people are put up against a wall, primal instinct kicks in, and they will do whatever is required to survive. But, Fatalier knew, underneath his expensive English suit, that he was a coward. Deep inside, he had a knowing feeling, one of moral decay. The possibility of his fraud being exposed had always been there.

A greater fear rose deep in his chest. She was the only one who could take it all away from him. Everything. He looked for a security guard or a police officer but could see none on the sidewalk or the surrounding areas. What would he say anyway? Arrest her? And for what crime? He knew that he would have to handle this matter discreetly. Since the war, he had rose to the top of his profession—he was a distinguished and respected banker; she was just a peasant girl. He reassured himself he could handle her.

As he moved into Post Office Square, Fatalier remembered the gun he kept in his bedside table at home in Hingham. It was next to the black velvet case that held his Purple Heart. He had another gun in a safe upstairs in his office at the bank—just in case someone came looking for him. Both were Lugers that he had acquired from an arms dealer in Charlestown when he arrived back in Boston from the war. He knew it was inevitable that someone would come looking for him, but he was shocked it was her. He was certain it would be the government. It seems that once you get on your feet in life, there is always someone who arrives on the scene to try to trip you up and put you out in the cold.

Fatalier looked to his left and glanced into the large glass window of a department store. as He saw her reflection following him quite closely. He made his way through the square and caught her image again in the window of a café. She wore a gray beret, a red scarf, and sunglasses in defiance of the cloudy Boston skies. He rounded the corner and headed out toward South Station, checking his watch as he went. It was now 5:15 PM. The 6:00 PM. commuter rail train would allow him to escape this nightmare, and he was determined to shake her before he got to the platform.

Fatalier saw a sign for The Ivy Club appear up ahead and felt a sense of relief. It was wedged between another bank and a restaurant—a men's only bar; she would not be allowed in. It was close enough to the station; he'd have a drink and make his train. He slipped through the door and felt relieved to be surrounded by male executives drinking whiskey and beer. He turned around and saw her looking at him through the window. There was vengeance in her eyes.

He pushed through the crowd, closer to the bar, and ordered a scotch and a shot of Jameson, which was brought rather quickly by the bartender. Fatalier was well-known at The Ivy Club and people respected him—he tipped handsomely. He kept his back to the window as he drank the whiskey and scotch down quickly, and his head was spinning deliriously. He thought of his wife and children waiting for him at home, unaware of who he truly was. A father is in many ways an actor, providing a strong, stable appearance for women and children, despite his vulnerabilities. However, standing here, Fatalier felt the curtains opening, exposing his charade. He had been a masquerader for fifteen years. If he was to run—again—he would somehow have to get back home to get his money and passport. All necessary precautions had been arranged long ago—just in case. He tapped the bar and signaled to the bartender that he was ready for another round as he felt the hand on his shoulder.

"Essex—what the hell are you doing here?" shouted a voice.

Fatalier turned to the voice calling his false name, and saw it was his boss, Russell Danforth, behind him. Relief ran through his body.

"Jesus, Danforth," he said. "You startled me."

"Are you okay, Essex?" Danforth asked. "You look pale."

Danforth and he had attended Harvard together. They were old friends. Fatalier was able to gain acceptance to the Ivy League school on a GI Bill that was made available to soldiers coming back from the war. Fatalier had used deceptive means. He had found a man in the North End, who was able to do that sort of thing. Birth certificates, legal documents, driver's licenses. Even a passport. Using his fake information, he was able to fraudulently fund his Ivy League education. He was able to leave his old, impoverished life behind and realize a new existence as David Essex.

Fatalier looked back at the window nervously. She was gone. For now.

"Essex, I didn't want to do this here," began Danforth.

"Do what?" asked Fatalier, nervously.

He felt his body shake with fervor but tried to not make it apparent.

"Give you some news," said Danforth.

"Right, news," said Fatalier, relieved for a moment. "What's up?"

"I'm leaving the bank. I've gotten an offer in London," said Danforth. "You'll be up for the presidency, pending clearance by the board. You'll be overseeing the bank operations, Essex. Congratulations."

Fatalier thought about his false name: David Essex. Lieutenant David Essex. Soon-to-be Bank President David Essex.

But David Essex was dead. Fatalier had killed him in France, by accident, of course. He was trying to save Essex from three Nazi soldiers, but it all went terribly wrong. And, the irony was, just hours before, Fatalier had made his decision to go AWOL, a decision that brought him upon Lieutenant Essex's pending execution on his path to cowardice and surrender. From behind, some brush, he did not see David Essex about to be hung, he instead saw himself. Perhaps they coincidentally resembled each other, but Fatalier felt his own neck in that noose. Despite his desertion, he had to help this man. He left the execution site and came upon the German's ammunition supply. Upon his return, he was able to toss several grenades close enough to kill the Nazis. However, Essex, took the worst of it. Miraculously, the French girl was able escape without injury. Delirious after the explosion that had killed all of them, he had inspected the carnage, he made the insane decision to take off Essex's dog tags and put them around his own neck. He then set his own dog tags next to the body of David Essex and his metamorphosis was complete.

It was that day that he took refuge at the cottage of the French girl—her parents had been hung by the Nazis due to their involvement with the French Underground, but she had stayed alive. It took weeks until the front fell and American troops found him at her home in that French Village. Lieutenant David Essex, so they thought, was still alive but wounded. Brent Fatalier was dead. Only, the French girl, Veronique, he suddenly recalled. She knew all about his crime.

"Cigarette?" Danforth asked, holding out a silver.

"Sure, thanks," he said, returning from his recollection.

Fatalier took one and Danforth lit it.

"They'll be a security clearance when you get the offer, just to make sure you aren't with the Russians," Danforth chuckled. "Where you'd say you were from?'

"Manhattan," Fatalier responded. "Grew up on the West Side."

Another lie. He was from Woonsocket, Rhode Island, and grew up in an orphanage run by Catholic nuns. When he turned sixteen, he'd run away and joined the Army when the Japs bombed Pearl Harbor: Brent Fatalier was his real name. He'd learned the New York accent when he was in England, bunking with a guy from Long Island. They were the paratroopers, the grunts, the first to arrive on D-Day in the darkness of night. They'd flown over to Normandy together. Last time he had seen him, they were about to jump out of a plane from a thousand feet. Fatalier imagined he was dead now, that he never survived the invasion past the first few moments...at least that's what he liked to think. He'd barely survived himself and still wore the mental battle scars to prove it.

"You see, the Feds check things out. New requirement thanks to McCarthy.... but you were in the service, right?" asked Danforth.

"Yes. 101st Airborne," he said.

"You're kidding me," blurted Danforth. "D-Day? You're a goddamn hero."

But Fatalier knew he was no hero. He was a fraud. He'd nearly defecated himself on the flight over from England on June 6, 1944, and, due to some psychological circumstances, he'd decided to go AWOL. When he landed behind enemy lines, half the men he jumped with were shot dead on the ground, killed by German machine guns. The sight of the carnage made things worse. He had abandoned his unit and walked toward the German side ready to surrender. His intention was to give up intelligence, it was his vengeance for this suicide mission they'd sent him on.

Danforth was distracted by someone who walked in, and Fatalier finished his cigarette, took out his wallet, and set some money on the bar for the drinks.

"Listen, Russ, I have to catch my train. You know how Margaret gets when I'm late for dinner," Fatalier said. "Congrats on London. We'll discuss this more tomorrow."

"Of course," said Danforth, shaking his hand.

There would be no discussion tomorrow, no bank presidency, or background check for Fatalier. He would be a fugitive again in just a few hours—he was surprised he had made it this far in the ruse. The plan was always to take the lie as far as it could go. To get some money in his pocket; he had not anticipated the $50,000 a year salary, a stately home in a bedroom community of Boston, a country club membership, an adoring wife and two children. He'd be halfway across the U.S. by noon tomorrow. There was no sense fighting it. He had enough saved to survive for a very long time. Of course, he accepted that he'd have to leave some of his fortune for Margaret and the children. He'd pay an attorney to file the divorce and write a comforting note. This was his day of reckoning and every detail had been thought out well in advance. When all was said and done, he would just become no one—a drifter with another false identity. He always knew this was his fate. It was never about if...only about when.

Fatalier pushed through the smoky bar and emerged out on the sidewalk. He took in a deep breath of the fresh air. She was not there. It started raining harder, and he walked briskly toward South Station, studying the people he passed. He was less nervous now after a few drinks and cigarettes. He had laid out his plan carefully. He was a man alone.

As he entered the station, he saw her. She had positioned herself on a bench by the entrance, awaiting his arrival. He froze. Should he run? The train was the fastest way home, and to his freedom. He looked over his shoulder to the street, but before he could move, she was in front of him.

"Nous retrouvons donc," she said firmly. "We meet again."

He knew some French, mostly French Canadian from Woonsocket.

"What do you want from me? Money?" Fatalier asked. "I can pay you."

He took out his wallet and took out some bills.

"You think this is about money?" she stammered.

She was older now. She was probably close to eighteen when he had met her. She had saved him from the Nazis. She had saved him from himself.

"You've done well for yourself, Mr. GI," she remarked. "Vice President. A wife and kids."

Fatalier studied her cautiously. He was sure she been following him for a while now. She knew details of his life, after all. He wondered if she had a weapon underneath her coat. He'd read a story in the *New Yorker* a few years back by John Cheever about a jilted secretary holding her boss at gunpoint when he fired her after their one-night love affair. But that was not the case in this situation. He knew he had harmed her. Theirs was an emotional love, mostly on her side—a crush.

"Tu m'as quitté. M'a abandonné," she said bitterly. "You abandoned me."

"I didn't abandon you," Fatalier insisted. "The Army sent me home. I had no choice. They don't let you take a French girl with you."

"I saw what you did," she said. "You took his identification tags… tags from his dead body."

"Yes. I did," Fatalier said.

"Vous estes un imposteur." she said. "Imposer."

"It was something I had to do. It changed my life. I was nothing before that. Just a poor orphan forced to go to war."

He looked up at the clock. It was closing in on 6:00 PM. He needed to get home and get the farewell letters he had written long ago from the safe, never mind the resignation letter from the bank. He knew his time was up in Boston and once he got rid of her—again—he could move forward with his existence. He waved the money at her.

"Take this. I must go home to my wife and children," he insisted. "My train will be leaving soon."

"This is about betrayal," she said. "To me and your country."

He stared down at her. She was still a beautiful girl, in her late twenties now. She could destroy him with her knowledge. Her motivation was strong. She wanted him to apologize for hurting her, he thought, that's all she wanted.

"I'm sorry," Fatalier finally said. "Is that it? I'm sorry I left you behind and broke your heart."

She looked at him sadly.

"C'est tout ce que je voulais entendere," she said. "This is all I wanted to hear."

"So, are we good now? May I go home?" asked Fatalier.

She stepped forward as if to kiss him, then pressed the gun to his navel. He looked at her horrified.

"Now we must finish this business. Buy me a ticket for the train," she said.

***

As he sat next to her, in the back carriage, he thought about all his sins and misgivings. What made a man commit evil? What if he had landed in France and killed twenty Nazis with his rifle? Would that have been better? Would he have been a hero then? If he had taken off his uniform and blended into French society, living his days out with her as his young French wife, would that have saved his soul?

Instead, he pretended to be a more affluent person. He faked his identity and went to Harvard and realized a life that no one else from the orphanage would have dared to dream of.

Veronique pressed the muzzle up against his ribs to remind him of his reality. The rest was all illusion. He sat up straight. He could probably take the gun away from her; he had been trained as a soldier.

She came closer and whispered. "I want to meet your wife," she said. "I want to see the life you chose without me."

He turned and stared at her. She was not right in the head. Perhaps the war had damaged her thinking. Like it had damaged his. She also wore her battle scars on the inside. What she was doing was not the actions of a sane woman. They did kiss and make love, but the affair in France was brief. She had cared for him. They had been able to hide from the Americans and Brits who had invaded the surrounding area, as he did not want to reveal his crimes. He had told her stories of America and was able to speak some French with her, but in the loneliness of war, they had had a physical relationship, albeit brief. He hated himself for that because she was much too young. He had just turned twenty-one and he was unsure of her age. If the affair had taken place in America today, and had there been a line crossed, he'd be brought up on charges—he was sure of that much. He was probably her first love. Fatalier empathized with her and her feelings of abandonment, but there was truly nothing he could do.

After a forty-five-minute ride, the train slowed to a halt. His wife would be waiting for him at the station in the Chevy station wagon, the same one that he would use the next day to depart from his life forever. The train jolted and he quickly stood up. She pressed the gun through her coat. He knew that he could use the crowd to escape, but as he considered that he saw a familiar face.

"Dave," shouted Chip Keating, an associate at the bank and his neighbor.

Fatalier always despised his small talk, but tonight he was excited to hear his voice.

"Well, you're coming home early!" he said. "Who is your friend?'

Fatalier looked back at Veronique, who shook her head as if to say, "Get rid of him!"

"Oh...this is our new... French exchange student," he exclaimed. "I just picked her up at Logan."

Keating studied her and chuckled.

"Right, right. Isn't she kind of old to be an exchange student?" he said.

"Yeah, well...she's in a graduate program at B.U.," responded Fatalier.

"Right," said Keating, winking at him. "Anyway, are we on for this weekend at the club?"

"For what?" Fatalier asked.

"The tournament? Golf?"

"Oh, yes. Right. I'll definitely be there," Fatalier said nervously.

Keating smiled.

"Good luck with your French girl," whispered Keating as he departed.

As they exited the train and walked down the platform, Fatalier saw Margaret sitting in the Chevy. It was too late to run now. Veronique was too unpredictable. He walked slowly and shamefully up to the window. Margaret rolled it down. He felt the muzzle right behind him against his lower back.

"Hello, dear," he said. "This young lady is coming to stay at our home this evening."

Margaret looked at Veronique.

"She's an intern with the Bank of France," he continued. "She just arrived today."

His wife looked at him skeptically.

"Well, I wish you would have called ahead, David," she said. "I would have put clean sheets in the guest room."

"I'm sorry, darling."

He opened the back door for Veronique, and she got in. He shut the door and realized for a moment it would be the perfect time to run. However, that thought was fleeting as he recalled all he needed to collect from home—that, and the fact that he wouldn't leave his wife alone with this unstable French woman. If only he could get to his gun. He would have to create a distraction to get to the drawer in his bedroom. He opened the passenger side door and got in. He felt her presence hovering behind him.

Margaret drove and began some small talk about her day, the gossip of the neighborhood, all the rumors floating around town. Fatalier tried to focus. His wife had nothing to do with his lies; she deserved better than this. He had met her in Cambridge at a Harvard-Radcliffe mixer. He liked her because she didn't seem like she was shopping for a rich, legacy Harvard man. She just wanted someone to make her laugh. Now, he had put her life in danger with his recklessness and deception. He knew he could make everything right tonight, but it would require her to be accepting of those sins.

"Darling, I have to tell you something," Fatalier interrupted.

"What is it?" she asked curiously.

He paused.

"David, what is it?"

Fatalier turned and looked at Veronique. She held the gun toward him. It became visible in the rearview mirror. He heard Margaret gasp when she saw it.

"Ne dis plus un mot," she stammered. "Stop this."

Fatalier ignored her.

"When I was in France in the war, I was wounded, and this young lady cared for me. This was long before we were married," he continued.

"Arrête Stop this!" Veronique said.

"My name is not David Essex, darling. My name is Brent Fatalier. I took a man's dog tags after a tragic accident, and I assumed his identity. Do you understand me?"

Margaret nodded slowly. She was obviously in shock.

"I'll shoot her if you don't shut up," Veronique said firmly.

It was at that point Fatalier decided to grab the gun away from her. He pushed his body back over the seat and grabbed it. He obviously startled her, and she pulled the trigger twice and the bullets struck Margaret in the back of the head. Horrified, Fatalier pushed her away and slid back over to grab the wheel of the car. They were in a remote part of town by the woods off Long Pond, and he was able to get his foot on the brake and stop the car. By the time it was over, Margaret was slumped back and lifeless. Blood covered the seat.

"You've killed her!" he screamed.

The girl was in shock, and she set the gun on the back seat.

"Is this what you came here to do? Kill my wife?" Fatalier screamed.

"Je suis désolé!" she screamed.

Fatalier's mind raced. What would he do? The police would ultimately pin this murder on him because he could not blame the French girl. She'd tell them everything about his abandonment.

He let Margaret fall sideways onto the front seat and opened the passenger side door. He got out and looked up. There was a harvest moon now floating in the sky. His deception and cowardice had killed the woman he had come to love. How selfish of him! He walked around to the driver's side and got in. He had no fear of the French girl now. He started the car and drove. He had made up his mind that he would dump the car in the pond after killing the French girl. He would not allow the children to see their mother in this state. He drove to his house and pulled it in the driveway.

"Stay here," he commanded. "I will be back in a moment."

She was weeping quietly in the back seat when he left her. Fatalier walked into the house. The children would be in their rooms. He did not want to see them again. He could not see them again. He walked to his office quietly and unlocked the safe. He took out his old documents, then found a briefcase and clicked it open. He placed three passports and a few thousand in cash in there. If he waited until morning, he could take the rest out of the bank, but it occurred to him that he should leave it for the children. He'd have to decide before the government or lawyers got involved. It could be done. He had that man in Charlestown who settled these matters discreetly. For a fee, of course.

Fatalier made his way quietly upstairs to the bedroom and found the gun and bullets in the drawer. He set the briefcase down on the bed, clicked it back open, and found the bullets, then loaded the Luger. He imagined this day of reckoning being much more hectic, but Fatalier had laid his plan out well, considering most of the obstacles that would be in his way. He paused but again, could not convince himself to say goodbye to the children.

***

Fatalier drove the car out to the quarry and parked. Veronique sat up and looked around.

"What are we doing here?" she asked.

"I'm going to dump the car and you are going to help me," he said. "And then we can be togther."

Their eyes met and Fatalier saw that there was a sense of belief. She was about to get what she came for, what she had lost so long ago in that French village in 1945.

He heard her get out the other side, and he exited after her. When she came closer, and without hesitation, Fatalier shot her twice in the head.

The gunshots echoed off the quarry and she fell to the ground. He picked up her lifeless body and tossed it over the ledge without remorse. He opened the door of the car and dragged Margaret's body out. She hadn't deserved this fate. A wave of sadness came over him as he tossed her body into the quarry. He had loved her and she didn't deserve this. Double homicide. Besides the accident with the Germans and his lieutenant, he hadn't killed anyone purposely in his life. Now, he was the executioner. He got back in the car, put it into drive, and did not look back.

***

Around Madison, Connecticut, he pulled over. He took out an envelope with a letter enclosed that he had written a few years ago and mailed it to his attorney. His second letter was to the man in the North End to ensure that the children would be cared for with the money he had hidden. The government would have to work hard to find it, but he felt that with his banking knowledge, it would be there for them. He dropped it in the mailbox at the rest area and got back in the car.

As he drove onto the George Washington Bridge, he felt himself starting to get tired. Very tired. He closed his eyes a time or two and knew how dangerous driving like this was, but he continued. The glowing Empire State Building rose above the city, and he smiled. Escape—it was his only goal. A strange tightness came in his throat, which he found quite odd. There was a tremendous pressure, like he had felt earlier in the elevator when he first saw her. He tried to loosen his red silk tie, but it defied him and tightened further. He closed his eyes and tried to fight for his breath.

When he opened them, all he saw was the face of the Nazi commander, Wilhelm Baumer, shouting, "Zieh ihn hoher hoch. Mac ihn fertig!" and from his study, it translated: "Pull him up higher! Finish him!"

Fatalier grabbed his throat as he looked down and saw the French girl watching him from below sadly. He pulled at the tightening noose and tried to scream for them to stop. They had the wrong man. He'd gone AWOL. He had not ordered the ambush. With the final tug, his neck snapped once and for all.

Brent Fatalier, or who they thought was Lieutenant David Essex was no more.

The Nazis gave a cheer and the commander motioned to bring him down. He went over to Fatalier's body and reached down and pulled off his dog tags.

"Ruhe in Frienden, Lieutenant David Essex."

Baumer looked around and shook his head, thinking of his wife and children, back in Berlin.

"Men do terrible things to each other in war," he said sadly. He took out a cigarette and a soldier lit it quickly. Wilhelm Baumer inhaled, then blew out a cloud of smoke. He studied the beauty of the French countryside littered with corpses of Germans and Americans sprawled around him, shaking his head at the strange juxtaposition before him as he realized exactly how terrible men can be when faced with life or death.

Diamond Bar

y dad has always had an affinity for diamonds and gold. That's why I'm not surprised when I pick him up at Walpole, he informs me about his "new plan." I've heard these words more than once in my life.

Interpretation: it's another heist.

"You see, Jimmy, if you lay out the plan very carefully and anticipate all the variables, it turns to gold," he says. "Anytime that I've gotten caught, something unexpected happened. You gotta think of every possibility."

He taps his index finger against his temple in a way that bothers me.

My whole life, my father has constantly told me that everything he touches "turns to gold." The reality is, that everything he has touched has turned to absolute shit. This is not his first time at Walpole.

I get a gnawing in my gut, the same one that has been there since I was kid. You know that one that questions your parents' decision-making ability? It's that feeling that my world is about to fall apart again—like it always does with matters concerning my dad.

I study the barbwire that runs around the prison. My eyes eventually meet up with the two guards, both holding rifles, and I can feel them staring at me through the dark lenses of their Ray-Bans—as if they are trying to send me a message. *Run away!* I shake the feeling off and start the car. As I drive, I feel as if I am escaping my fate—for now.

The truth is that more than one member of my family has lodged at Walpole at one time or another—so it stands to reason that I would logically be next. We are a traditional criminal family. My uncle was in here for a few years for armed robbery, and believe it or not, my cousin and my aunt too, for lesser charges but bad enough to land in prison. And, by my count, my father has checked in and out three times since I was a kid. A decade in the slammer is a long time.

"So, whatcha been up to, Jimmy-boy?" my dad asks as he sits in the passenger seat of my new-used '79 Grand Marquis.

"Not much," I say. "Started my own landscaping business."
"Nice," he says. "My boy's an entrepreneur. Regular Jeff Bezos, he is. Growing your business, huh?"

"Yep," I say. "I've got about twenty lawns now."

"Beautiful. Feels good to put the green stuff in your pocket, huh?"

Growing things is one of my more redeeming qualities. I think it's deep-rooted in my Irish DNA; although, I've never actually been to Ireland. On the weekends, after work, I watch one of those gardening shows on Netflix. Seems that all the Irish and English people head out to the garden in front of their houses and start digging when they have problems. It's like some form of therapy for them to dig in the soil and try to grow shit. On this one show, this old-timer, who was about eighty, was digging for hours, then stopped for tea, and ended up at the local pub talking about his beautiful roses and begonias. I guess he'd been a soldier in the IRA at one point or another and talked about how it was therapeutic because all the Catholics were blowing up the Protestants and vice versa. Duality of man. Evil turns to good. He said he's a better person now.

My grandfather came off the boat from Ireland and ended up in Boston in the 1930s, looking for a new opportunity. Unfortunately, he was discriminated against—which, according to him, happened to all the Irish back then. Signs said, "Irish Need Not Apply." Between planting flowers, one time when I was a kid, he explained that our family got caught up in organized crime—which he sincerely regretted. He told me that the Irish had no other choice because society hated them, and an "opportunity" had to be created.

Later in life, I figured out how to make money using my gardening skills because my family had little money. Due to my father's gambling, drinking, and frequent incarcerations, my grandfather had to raise me, and my dad was more like an older brother to me, not a father. His drinking split our family up and, eventually, my mom abandoned me when she took off for California, since my dad was always getting locked up. She apparently couldn't take it anymore. My grandfather legitimized the family, and finally opened a flower shop in Brighton. He was embarrassed by my dad. He wanted a different path for me because my father always taught me to destroy things. It was as if my old man took pleasure in the chaos and destruction that he loved to regale as being *turned to gold*.

Ever since my grandfather died a few years back, I have contemplated which direction I was going to go in life as a man...but just like a fox with his tail on fire, my family makes me run back to all those predictable places. I could go either way in my mind; I was currently undecided.

My father grabs my pack of Camels in my cupholder and lights one. I drive up Route 1A, then up to Route 1, past Gillette Stadium. For some reason, I think about the article I read about that New England Patriot murderer, Aaron Hernandez, and him being able to hear the loudspeakers from Patriot games as he sat alone in his prison cell at Walpole. And I sort of want to ask my dad if that's possible or not, but I don't.

"What else? Tell me everything you've been up to," says my father. "You didn't call too much while I was in the slammer."

"I've been busy," I say. "Been going to school too. Taking classes at the community college. Massasoit. English."

"Fantastic. I always loved that James Joyce fella. Paralysis, delirium, escape and what not. Your grandfather liked all that

Irish literature. He used to read it to me as a kid. It is some pretty depressing shit," my dad says as he sucks in the smoke.

He suddenly gets serious for a moment.

"Listen, Jimmy, there's been a little change in plans."

I'm not surprised. My whole life there has always been "a change in plans." I knew it was inevitable. First time he got out of Walpole, on a furlough program that liberal governors put in place, it was a trip down to Foxwoods. He had a guy in Pawtucket who was able to manipulate the GPS on his ankle bracelet to make it look like he was at the church half the time he was on furlough.

Divine Intervention of the illegal kind.

Of course, that night, my dad ended up walking out of the casino with $10,000 in cash and four pounds of gold that he won in a back-room poker game.

I spent most of the weekend playing roulette by myself, as I always do. Later, I ended up hooking up with a pretty bartender in our comped room. Back-room card games were not interesting to me. But she had been.

I look at my father, shake my head, and sigh.

I recall that less than two months later, he had gambled away all the money and was back at Walpole after a botched bank robbery in Brockton. My dad could always dream up a big heist, but he struggled with the final execution. Kind of a family curse.

"Where are we going this time?" I ask, bracing for the answer. "I ain't driving all the way to Connecticut again."

"Martha's Vineyard," he says proudly.

I nod, trying to remain unfazed. For once, in a long-time, his words sounded appealing to me.

I've never been to The Vineyard, which is ironic, because my hometown, New Bedford, is a forty-five-minute ferry ride—twenty-three nautical, or twenty-six aerial miles—to the island. I remember standing in the harbor as a kid, looking through some binoculars he bought me at Savers, watching yachts and boats go by, headed off to Nantucket or The Vineyard. The islands were on the map but were too far away to see from shore.

"You see, my cell mate, this guy, Jose Correia, tells me about this boat he was on that sank a few years back. He said it was loaded with diamonds and gold coins and bars," my dad explains. "Maybe a cool mill worth."

I shake my head pessimistically and drive-up Route 495 until I hit the junction of Route 24. My dad smokes a couple more Camel Blues as we listen to the Sox game. They are losing. I decide to flip stations, and Robbie Dupree sings "Steal Away" followed by "The Wreck of the Edmund Fitzgerald" by Gordon Lightfoot. Although I like the old stuff, I get depressed and turn it down and soak in some quiet. He finally directs me to pull off in Taunton, so he can go to Walmart to buy a burner phone. When he's done, he makes me drive to a triple-decker where his buddy lives. He's in there for twenty minutes and comes out with a backpack and a bottle of Jameson and two Glocks, which he puts in the glovebox.

"Let's head up to the harbor. We got a boat to catch. You ever been scuba diving, Jimmy?" he asks.

I don't reply. I've learned not to question any part of his 'plan'. I continue to drive because this is all I know. I get a year or two hiatus from my dad's destructive personality every time he goes in the freezer; I will forever be a convict's son. Self-fulling prophesy. I continue to drive because today is my day off and I've got nothing else to do...besides, crime will keep me out of the bar. That's where I go when I'm not growing things. It's a place that is dark and quiet, and the alcohol numbs my pain. Days off are a torture because my DNA, deep down inside my cell nuclei and mitochondria, is programed for addiction and criminal tendencies. My dad is my only family left. Everyone else is dead or relocated to California, to get away from the cold, the depression, and bad memories. As I drive down the long, horizontal stretch of 140, I think about palm trees and beaches, girls in bikinis and writing a movie script, then in another fantasy, the Irish countryside or wandering around London. I think about if I had enough money to get out of here, I'd do it and go live life on my own terms. I would tell those rich customers, the ones who complain about the fungus and weeds in their grass, to fuck off. As I drive, I wish I could get so rich—once and for all, so I could tell them all to go to hell.

The seemingly endless state highway finally curves onto Interstate 195, and I take the downtown exit to the harbor, pull into the ferry lot, and pay a kid $15 for parking.

"We are parking here but we got to switch cars to keep our profile low," my dad says.

He gets out and makes a few phones calls on his burner phone, and fifteen minutes later, a blue '85 Cadillac Eldorado pulls up.

"This is your Uncle Ziggy," my dad says. "He refurbishes Caddies. Fuckin' obsessed them."

I don't have an Uncle Ziggy, but the Eldorado looks to be in mint condition.

I get in the back seat and my dad sits up from on the burner phone calling his "colleagues."

"You got a diver?" Ziggy asks.

"Yeah, we got a diver," my dad says. "Who do you think I am... Jacques Cousteau?"

"How much we talkin'?" asks my new uncle.

"None of your fuckin' business, Zig," my dad shouts.

"I was just askin'," he retorts defensively.

"Yeah, well, you better keep your eyes on the road. Distracted drivin'. You ever heard of that?"

"Just askin."

"Listen, Zig. You are getting compensated very well. This ain't charity work; you are getting paid here. Maybe someday you can hold the bullets and call the shots. For now, I'm due reparations because I'm the one who took the rap for Brockton. I served my time for you bastards on that bank job, and I didn't snitch on none of you."

We pull up at the dock.

"Remember what they say, Zig: Snitches get stitches. Remember that," my dad says sternly. "Keep your phone close. Pick us up when I call. I got debts to pay. Never know if we'll have collateral damage out on the mighty sea."

I walk up the dock and study the harbor. There are a ton of private vessels, and yachts. Farther down the dock, I study the larger fishing vessels, the ones with long masts. The location is unbelievable: under ninety minutes to Nantucket and forty-five minutes to Martha's Vineyard.

"This is the one," my dad says, pointing to a rather beat-up boat.

I look at the side of the boat: It reads: *The Albatross*. My dad laughs.

"Rhyme of the fuckin Ancient Mariner," he says. "Don't shoot the seagulls, Jimmy-boy. We'll all be cursed."

It's a small vessel and I hesitantly board. My dad sets the bottle of Jameson down and reaches in his backpack and takes out a second Glock and hands it to me.

"I know watcha thinkin'. Just in case anyone tries to fuck us over," he says softly.

I tuck mine in the back of my jeans.

"Let's have a drink," he declares.

He finds two glasses and pours the bottle of Jameson. I put mine down quickly and the burn feels good. I turn to see a very muscular, very tan man walking toward us with scuba gear in his hands.

"Diamonds?" the man says in broken English.

My father glares at him.

"Shut the fuck up and get on here," he scolds.

My dad starts up the boat and backs out of the harbor. I never knew he could operate one. I don't recall him taking me on a boat ride in my lifetime, especially one this nice.

It's still daylight, and we head out on the Acushnet River out to Buzzards Bay. My dad guides the boat and laughs.

"You ever read *Moby Dick*, Jimmy?"

"Yeah," I yell over the motor. "Twice."

"Captain Fucking Ahab!" he shouts.

I don't join him in his laughter because in many ways, I feel like Melville's character, Ishmael, at this moment. I am the son, the one who is tortured by his past and afraid of his future, due to the father planning this fated mission. Like the biblical Ishmael, I feel like my father would sacrifice me to fill his thirst for wealth. Tonight, I am headed to sea, but I feel like I've been wandering in the desert for the last twenty years with no oasis or providence in sight.

My dad pulls up his sleeve and studies some coordinates he has written in black Sharpie on his left arm. I recall his earlier words: "Jimmy, if you lay out the plan very carefully, and anticipate all the variables, it all turns to gold."

"70 degrees 44 and 41 degrees 04," says my dad. "Okay, Kino. Let's go."

"My name's not Kino...call me Sanchez, amigo."

My father starts laughing.

"Okay, Sanchez," he shouts over the motor. "Get ready to dive for treasure."

"It's getting dark," says Sanchez. "We started out way too late. Is not safe, señor. Sharks come out."

I look out to the west and the sun is falling quickly. I study the darkening waters ahead and I think about the sharks waiting for us at the diamond bar.

"Listen, you need to dive down about 150 meters. There is a sand bar that this ship clipped. Had rocks or something sharp stuck in it, ripped the bow wide open. Sunk like a block of cement. My cellmate tells me that there's a chunk of change down there—Davy Jones's fuckin' locker. We'll be watching you and I'll send the cage down to pick up what you find."

Sanchez looks at him, then me.

"And I'm making $5000 off this?" he asks.

"Yeah. Cash. That was the deal," said my dad. "Another $5000 if we hit the jackpot down there. Plus, your silence, mi amigo."

Sanchez finishes suiting up, and sits down on the edge of the boat, then plunges into the ocean. My dad pulls out a steel cage basket and brings it to the side of the boat, then lowers it into the water. Sanchez pulls it down with him.

"Come on and look at this crazy ass technology shit," my old man says.

I follow him back into the cabin and he points to the screen. I see the video view from inside the cage as it descends toward Sanchez, who is diving downward with his light shining outward as he dives deeper and deeper. Then, the sandbar appears about one-hundred meters below the surface.

"There it is!" my old man cries with glee. "Jimmy, I told you!"

I looked closer and there was the yacht wedged into the sandbar.

"Holy shit," I say. "There it is."

"You see, it was cruising along and caught some rocks. My cellmate, he was with these guys, running guns, drugs, diamonds, and gold from Miami. He ends up jumping overboard—hell, maybe he was pushed—and some of his crew went down with the ship. He was able to stay afloat, but the Coast Guard picked him up in the middle of the Atlantic, and he got locked up with me in Walpole. Can you believe that shit?"

I shake my head. I see him disappear into the yacht, then come up with a walkie-talkie in his hand.

"Sanchez—can you hear me?"

"Yeah. I found some gold bars. I'll put them in the basket of the cage."

"Is there a safe?"

"Dunno. Let me go back in."

He disappeared on the sonar for a few minutes. My dad pulls the basket and cage up. As it comes to the surface, he beams, like a proud father.

"Gold! I can't fucking believe it," he screams. "The bastard was telling the truth!"

It takes another hour, but the stack of gold gets higher and higher with each delivery of bars. Finally, we see Sanchez crack the safe, and bags and bags of diamonds rise like a phoenix out of the ocean.

I look at my old man. It's the happiest I've ever seen him in my life. Tears run down his face. Five years in prison has apparently made him sentimental.

"Sanchez," he says over the radio. "Anything else?"

"No. That looks like that's it," he replies.

"Okay, come on up," my dad says.

He looks at me and smiles.

"Now I can retire, Jimmy. No, I can live an honest life off this heist. Who says crime doesn't pay, my boy?" he declares.

I resent the fact that calls me "boy." I hear Sanchez surface in the darkness. Night has fallen, and my dad points the spotlight down in the water directly onto Sanchez's face.

I don't see my father pull the gun until it's too late. Three quick shots hit Sanchez's forehead. I shine my flashlight toward where the shots went and see the blood combine like oil with the salt water—then, Sanchez is gone. My dad points the flashlight back at my face, and I realize I am an accomplice in not only this robbery, but a murder now.

"We good here, Jimbo?"

I nod.

"Yeah. We're good, Dad," I say.

"Okay, let's head back to shore," my dad says.

It takes an hour or so before I can see the lights of New Bedford in front of us. The ride back seemed longer than the ride there. But maybe that's my guilt over what I just witnessed. I think of Sanchez's dead body floating out into the abyss as the shark's circle and devour him for their dinner. Poor bastard never saw it coming. Neither did I.

But I guess I should've seen it coming. Desperation and diamonds are a motivating force for my father.

Poor Sanchez. All that for a promise of $5000, and he got three bullets in the brain.

A few minutes later, we pull into the harbor. Uncle Ziggy is waiting in the El Dorado at the end of the dock.

"How'd it go?" asks Ziggy.

My father tells him to pop the trunk.

"Nothing. Just a bunch of seaweed and dead fish out there, Zig?" he says.

"What's in the bags?" he asks. "You got something, didn't you?"

"How about none of your fucking business."

"Hey, and where's that diver?" asks Ziggy.

"What are you…a reporter from *The Boston Globe* or some shit? Drive us to Friendly's in Dartmouth. I'm starving, I need a patty melt, some fries, and a Fribble."

I get in the back seat, and my father in the front. Ziggy drives out to Route 6, and I wonder when the Coast Guard is going to find Sanchez's body floating out there. Or will the sharks find it first? We pull up to Friendly's and get out.

"I'm going to get a patty melt and a happy ending—sundae, that is," says my dad as he laughs at his prison humor. We get out and go in and eat. I didn't realize how hungry I was as we dig into our greasy meal. Who knew that tension and murder were an appetite stimulant?

Ziggy looks at my father.

"I want my cut, Jack," he says. "Don't fuck me over. I know you got something out there."

My dad smiles at Ziggy.

"When did I ever fuck you over, Zig?"

"The Attleboro bank job for one. I never said a word when they picked me up. I even sent them down the wrong trail. Cost me a year at Old Colony," Ziggy says.

My dad shakes his head and takes out his wallet. He pays for the meal with a hundred-dollar bill and gets up.

"Let's go, Zig. I'll pay you when we get back to Taunton. The Silver City, as they call it. I gotta pay this guy. He ain't fooling around."

The drive down Route 140 isn't too long, but my dad tells Ziggy to pull over to the rest stop so he can take a leak.

Ziggy gets out too. They disappear into the darkness, then I hear two gun shots. My dad comes back to the car.

"Come on," he says. "We got to bury the body in the woods."

I drag a man, whom I only know as my Uncle Ziggy, deep into the woods and ask myself when this is going to stop. When I get back to the car, my dad directs me to continue the drive back to Taunton, to the same triple-decker, while my dad decides to give me some life advice.

"Jimmy, listen to me. I've been meaning to tell you for a while that I've been a terrible father to you. That's why I'm leaving. For good."

"Where are you going?" I ask softly.

My disappointing childhood flashes through my brain. Back to all my father's schemes and the chaos it brought me.

"I ain't never been to Europe. Always wanted to go there, like Rome or Paris or some shit. Down at Walpole, during our TV time, I used to watch that Rick Steeves guy at television time. He was always traipsing through some European village or drinking beer in a pub in

London or something. When you're locked up, you get delirious, and you start dreaming about escape. You're paralyzed in there, Jimmy. They cage you up when you're a criminal. But you're still a human being with dreams. No matter what mistakes you've made."

I nod. I understand how he arrived here. This was his last chance to escape his miserable existence.

He gets out of the car and tells me to pop the trunk. He hands me two gold bars and a handful of diamonds. He keeps the rest for himself.

"Get out of here. Make a life for yourself. Don't end up like me. Mowing lawns and raking leaves is no way to live," he says. "This will give you freedom. Go live. Don't be chasing that white whale I've been chasing my whole life."

I look up with him, astounded.

"Yeah, this English professor was my cellmate at Walpole for a bit. Literary criticism lectures daily. Made me read Melville," he says.

He pats my hand and I watch as he disappears into the triple-decker. I know it will be the last time I will see him. I put the car into drive and remember my car is back at the ferry lot, and that the first order of business is that I must get rid of Uncle Ziggy's car... but my fingerprints are all over it. I find a dirt road off Route 140, somewhere in Middleboro, and find a lake, where I decide to put the evidence in neutral and roll it in.

Less than an hour later, an Uber picks me up on Route 36 at a diner and takes me back to the city. As I see the lights of the city, I realize that I am a fox with his tail on fire running back to all the usual places. I find the Grand Marquis and drive it back home to my apartment in the South End. I go inside and set the diamonds and gold on the table and watch them glimmer and glow underneath the kitchen light, but they mean nothing to me. I know the cops will be looking for me soon—it's in my blood, after all—but I am exhausted and feel myself falling into deep sleep.

***

The next morning, I wake up on the couch and rub my eyes...my head kills. The gold and diamonds are still there, but all I need is coffee. I make a pot and click on the radio and listen to the news like I always do.

"Breaking story this morning: A murder in Taunton last night. A fifty-five-year-old man, who had just been released from Walpole Prison yesterday, was found executed in Massasoit State Park. State Police believe that he is connected to the murder of a diver who was found by the U.S. Coast Guard cutter off the coast of New Bedford early this morning..."

I listen to the end of the report and realize that my dad was set up by his cellmate to go find the diamonds and gold for him. His finder's fee was a few bullets to the head. He suffered the same fate that Sanchez did and, just like Sanchez, never saw it coming.

I go in my room and find a suitcase and pack it. I know that the cops will be looking for me eventually—they always do. I sit down with my laptop and find the earliest departure to London out of Logan. I do all the calculations, and estimate I have enough landscaping cash saved to buy a ticket. The diamonds and gold will carry me for a while until the delirium fades—and I know it will fade—it always does.

As I sit and type, I realize that my dad's affinity for diamonds and gold wasn't a bad thing for me after all.

In fact, they bought me my freedom.

The Collection

My Catholic faith has always been strong, but I have never allowed it to interfere with my job or my ethical judgment—until a year ago.

And let it be known that by all accounts, the late Father Stephen McKenzie was a pious man who made some immoral and unethical decisions. However, what I've come to realize, as I've gotten older, is that there is liability in blindly agreeing with popular opinion. It can eventually lead to great regret once proven false.

Perhaps this all began because of my nearly perfect attendance at Mass, or maybe it was my youthful face at forty years old. It was clearly the face of a former altar boy, perhaps this had led me to becoming Father McKenzie's confessor.

Some of the sins he confessed I will take to the grave, not because I wanted to protect him, but rather that I despise bad people walking free when they are the true criminals. Growing up in Rhode Island, then later Massachusetts, the number of clergies, politicians, embezzling businessman, and even everyday citizens who have been able to escape without indictment was beyond my comprehension.

His confession began, ironically, at an Irish pub called Finnegan's Wake, after 5 PM, one Sunday.

Due to the nature of my work, I was often forced to attend at that time because I worked overnight on Saturdays and usually slept in late Sunday morning. It was widely known by all parishioners that Father McKenzie enjoyed the temperate summer days as his family had a home on the coast. He would often invite a Jesuit from Boston College to come out to the suburbs and say Sunday morning masses, and he spent the day at the beach, soaking up the sun. Father McKenzie knew how to enjoy life, possibly because he had come to the priesthood later in life. He had turned fifty this year and he still maintained his fitness with jogging and kept a healthy tan. And although he had taken a vow of poverty, he kept his Mercedes in the garage by the rectory.

"I've been stealing from the church," he stated bluntly, after a sip of Guinness.

It took a moment to digest this confession, to comprehend his earth-shattering words. I picked up my pint and swallowed down half of my own Guinness.

"Father, you realize that you are informing me of a crime and...."

He held up his hand.

"I realize your position, and I know that that there will be legal consequences."

"For how long?" I inquired.

"Ten years," he said. "Give or take."

I motioned to the bartender, Mick.

"Two shots of Jameson, Mick."

I turned back at Father McKenzie, still stunned.

"You're the only person who knows," he said. "This is the first time I've admitted this to anyone."

"Ten years," I said. "That has to be...."

"$546,000," said Father McKenzie without hesitation. "Give or take."

I thought about the collection basket. Sure, there were some envelopes in there, but his figure seemed exaggerated.

"From the collection basket alone?"

"Yes, but also family donations. The Keneally's gave us $100,000 a few years back," he said. "It was for upgrades to the rectory."

"But those actually got done," I recalled. "The back porch, the bathrooms, and the roof."

Father McKenzie nodded.

"I had my brother do most of the work. I paid him something, but he thought he was being charitable. He's very Catholic."

Mick placed the shots down on the bar.

"What's the occasion, gents?"

"The end of the summer," I quickly responded, taking my shot, and handing Father McKenzie his.

It was more like the end of the innocence. I cautiously tapped his shot glass and we put them down swiftly. The Irish whiskey burned my throat but helped me cope with news of the confession.

I finished my pint and signaled to Mick for another one.

"So why are you telling me this, Father? You realize I have an obligation to turn you in. I can't cover this up," I said.

"Nor do I want you to," he responded. "I just need your expertise on how I go about getting out of this."

"Getting out of this? This is grand larceny, Father," I said firmly.

Mick set a second Guinness in front of me. I quickly grabbed it and took a long, hard swig. Mixed with the Jameson, I felt the burn.

"There's something else," he added. "I'm being blackmailed."

I felt my blood pressure rise, a throbbing in my temple. I was glad I was still jogging in my free time, otherwise his confessions just might have given me a stroke.

"Blackmailed?"

"Do you know Mrs. Lynch?" Father McKenzie asked.

"Of course. She lives on Stanley Street, near the church."

"Well, you must also know her husband has had some health setbacks."

I was aware of this. Her husband had taken a fall on his way up to Communion one Sunday evening. The EMTs came and took him away. Rumors were that it was early Parkinson's, but others said it was multiple sclerosis. They had moved to town a year ago and started attending Mass on a regular basis. They kept to themselves, but Mrs.

Lynch always seemed to avoid eye contact with me, especially if I had come straight from work.

"Mrs. Lynch has been blackmailing me," he said. "She was helping out around the church office when Mrs. McGee had her surgery. She must've gotten into the financial records and saw something was off with our accounts."

I nodded.

"So, she confronted you?"

"Not exactly. She came and met with me at the rectory about the financial needs of her husband's new condition. She had hoped that we might make a charitable 'donation'."

"How much?"

"All of it," Father McKenzie said.

"$546,000?"

"To the penny," he said. "She put it together somehow. Fired a shot across the bow to let me know that she knew."

I looked at my phone for a second, it was 6:30. I had to go pick up my kids, and my ex-wife would be worked up if I was late for the 7 PM Sunday night hand-off.

"Listen, Father. I want you to hold tight with this information for now. By the way, where is all this money?"

"Do you know about Bitcoin?"

"Yeah."

"Well, I did some investing," he said.

I shook my head in disappointment.

"I think you need an attorney...now. Also, about the blackmail issue...I need to interview Mrs. Lynch and we will talk about your options tomorrow," I said.

"Bless you, son."

"No, Father...don't bless me. I need to say a prayer for you. This is a federal crime."

I threw down two twenties on the bar and thought about the FBI rolling into my suburban town to arrest my parish priest for embezzlement.

"Please, let me..."

"No, Father. Your money is all tied up. Remember?" I said, shaking my head in disappointment. I didn't want to be tied into anything involving money with this man.

I had to get out of there. Too many eyes and ears all around.

***

My ex-wife lives on the polished, upscale side of town now; she had gotten what she wanted out of me with the alimony I paid. The worst part of our divorce was that she got together with my ex-partner, Rex Gammell...that bastard. As I pulled the squad car into the driveway of their new house, which he surely paid for with his overtime details, I saw her waiting on the steps. They hadn't tied the knot yet—probably because the ink wasn't quite dry on our divorce, but they were surely headed to the altar. She was waiting with my kids, a suitcase, and their backpacks. Guess she didn't want to waste a moment with small talk. I had them at my condo from Sunday night to Wednesday night.

"At the pub with priest again? How many pints did you have this time?" she asked, sniffing me.

"I didn't realize you were counting, Vanessa, but I know how you like to do that with the alimony, so I shouldn't be surprised," I quipped.

The kids ran out and hugged me as I popped the trunk of my cruiser.

"By the way, do you have my check?" she asked.

"Yeah, I have your check," I said, quite annoyed. I took it out of my shirt pocket.

She unfolded it, studied it, and nodded.

"Just watch the drinking," she said. "I don't want my kids getting hurt due to your poor judgment."

***

When we got back to my condo, the kids got caught up in a Disney movie and I grabbed my laptop and logged into the crime database. Father McKenzie's embezzlement was certainly startling, but something brought me back to Mrs. Lynch's evasive eyes, apparent blackmail, and shakedown of a corrupt priest.

I ran her information, but nothing came up on the criminal side, just a couple of traffic violations, but strangely enough, those violations happened in various parts of the country: Santa Monica, California; Boulder, Colorado; and Vero Beach, Florida. Odd. It appeared the Lynches had moved around frequently. It stood to reason that most elderly people with health issues would have settled in.

That was the first red flag for me.

People typically move around frequently because they are on the run from something—yourself, perhaps—but most likely criminal activities, like bad check writing, fraud, shoplifting, the list goes on and on.

And in most cases, cops should focus on the crime at hand because you wouldn't have one confession without the other. Father McKenzie was going to do some prison time—that was a given—but I saw two things going on: a priest who was, yes, a friend, but who had made some very bad decisions. However, there was the parishioner, who made some even worse decisions. Cops around the country have seen this in celebrity cases: someone does something immoral and illegal (sexual harassment, perhaps) but then is blackmailed by the alleged victim for large sums of money. No one is re-inventing the wheel here.

Of course, the right thing would have been to turn Father McKenzie in immediately and stepped away from this case due to conflict of interest, but I assure you, it was not my Catholic faith that made me hesitate. Instead, I believe it was Mrs. Lynch who blinded my judgment

Truly, it bothered me because she knew I was a trusted parishioner and a friendly officer from town. She surely read the paper when I had been awarded "Officer of the Year" for the Commonwealth after cracking the case on the NFL football player who murdered his friend. The ensuing investigation that I was part of led to us finding out that he also moonlighted as a gang member.

Yeah, that was me. I was known for enforcing for the law.

However, I found myself empathizing with my priest friend, who had never been involved with any type of illegal activity. At least none that I knew of. If he could just return the money, perhaps all would be well—but in my heart and with my knowledge of the law, I knew this was not a reality.

I closed my laptop and got the kids to bed. We'd all be up early for school. And I'd be meeting with Mrs. Lynch in the morning—just not the way I thought.

***

I drove my kids to school in the cruiser and dropped them off in front of their elementary school. Mrs. Smith was working traffic control in her tennis outfit, and she gave me a smile and a wave. I rolled down the window.

"Is that appropriate attire for the traffic monitor?" I joked.

"Oh, Officer, you'll have to handcuff me and take me away in your cruiser," she joked.

"See you Wednesday?" I asked.

She was newly divorced as well. We'd gone to high school together, and I'd taken her to the prom. My ex-wife never liked her because she felt she was too flirty and "dressed like a slut." I was told to stay away from her many a time. However, I walked the line for ten years, and in the end, it was my ex-wife who was the cheater.

I was over it now. I was a free man. And could hang out with whomever I pleased, and Mrs. Smith definitely pleased me.

I drove directly to the station to check in. I parked the cruiser and walked in the back door and down the hallway past the Chief's office. He caught sight of me as I passed by.

"Finn, in here, now," he barked.

I turned around and entered the office. Much to my surprise, sitting before me was Mrs. Lynch.

"Hello," I stammered, shocked to see her.

"Sit down, Finn," said the Chief.

I took a seat and felt my blood pressure increase.

"Mrs. Lynch here has some concerns about some issues over at St. Feehan's Parish. You belong over there, correct?"

"Yes, sir," I said. "What seems to be the problem?"

"Well, apparently her husband took a fall over there a few months ago. He tripped on a piece of carpet and injured himself quite badly. She mentioned you were at the Mass."

"Sure was. I made the call from my phone and attended to him while we were waiting for the EMTs," I said.

"Well, she's considering a lawsuit," the Chief continued.

"Against?"

"You, the department, the EMTs, fire department, the church, and possibly the town."

I nodded. I was careful when I approached the fallen Mr. Lynch for this very reason, and consciously did not move his body. The climate of law enforcement these days caused me to hesitate and wait for the EMTs to do their job.

"He is permanently injured from that day," Mrs. Lynch stated bitterly. "And you had something to do with it."

"Now, take it easy, Mrs. Lynch. Officer Finn is here voluntarily. This isn't a court room. We are three people having a reasonable discussion."

"Well, maybe you should keep a closer eye on your officers, Chief," she yelled. "Do you approve of them driving drunk in their cruisers?"

I looked at her, astonished. Was she following me? The Chief's face seemed to turn to stone, and he turned to me.

She reached in her purse and took out her phone, then held it up to him.

"My daughter works over at The Chieftain, that Irish pub by the stadium. She texted me this photo."

The Chief took the phone and studied the photo. He held it up to me.

"Care to comment?"

It was a still shot of Father McKenzie and me downing the Jameson shots. Four pints of empty Guinness were on the bar. Mick was a lazy bartender and never cleared his bar space, the bastard.

"She thought it was strange that a police officer was getting drunk with a priest."

I looked at her and she stared back at me. She knew that I knew everything. I was an obvious and trusted friend for Father Flynn to run to for help. The game was on. Checkers and chess playing at its finest. She was good, but I would win in the end. It occurred to me just then that she had done this before—many times before, in multiple states. She was practiced in the art of deception. A professional grifter.

"Mrs. Lynch, I'm going to ask you to leave the room at this point as I would like to have a word with Officer Finn," he said sternly. "Official police business."

She looked at me with one of those smirks that most of society would agree qualifies for an open hand slap. She got up slowly and, as she left the room, allowed her purse to hit my arm. She was sending a message. This was the warning shot.

The Chief got up and shut the door.

"Badge and gun. You are on leave, pending investigation, Finn."

"Chief, there's much more to this story," I said. "You have to hear me out."

He looked at me. We had a past, and I knew what he could do to defiant and disobedient officer's careers. He knew my history with the bottle—it had gotten me in trouble once before. I was wise enough not to argue. Slowly, I set both on his desk.

"Officer Finn, I am advising you to call your union representative if you want to discuss this further," he said. "I can have a fellow officer drop you off at home."

I shook my head. I despised his formal, patronizing tone. I wanted to scream at him what a fool he was, but I knew better. Once I had the evidence, he would come to his senses.

"No, thanks, Chief," I said firmly. "I'll take an Uber."

***

The hardest call I made that morning was to my ex-wife.

"Can you pick the kids up at school?" I asked. "Something has come up at work."

"What the fuck, Michael?"

"It's kind of serious. I got suspended."

"What did you do this time? More drinking?" she screamed.

"It's a long story."

"I'll bet. We just checked in to the hotel on The Cape," she screamed

"I'm sorry," I said in the phone. "It's a complicated situation."

Her voice was yelling on the other end, and I eventually hung up. I located my laptop and tried to log on but, of course, my privileges had been suspended to the crime database.

A few hours later, I went out to the garage and found my old mountain bike and rode over to the rectory. I knocked on the door, but no one answered. I took out my cellphone and realized I hadn't turned in my police-issued device. The Chief forgot. However, it occurred to me that they could track me with it, I knew that much. That was why it was no surprise when my ex-partner pulled up in his cruiser.

"What's up, Mike?" Rex said.

He was a tall, muscular guy, having gotten into CrossFit a few years back.

"I thought you were on The Cape," I said.

"Yep. Beth drove back and got the kids. I decided to pick up a shift since I had the cruiser down there."

It made sense. Beth was at home; he might as well pick up some overtime. Greedy bastard, he always was.

"What are you doing over here at the rectory? You are suspended."

"Yeah," I admitted. "Just trying to track down Father McKenzie.

"Funny thing is, we are too. Apparently, he's gone missing. The church secretary said he never came home last night. Know anything about that? Heard you guys were drinking buddies," Rex fired back.

Rex knew about my drinking because he was right there with me at the pub—he was no altar boy himself. We were young when we were matched up as partners. We met girls frequently while on patrol. I just found Vanessa first and he was, quite honestly, always a little jealous since he had his eye on her too.

And there was the issue of the shooting that occurred five years ago, the one that both of us would take to the grave. No matter how he betrayed me, that was a sworn secret for life. However, there were other ways for him to haunt me.

"Guess some money's gone missing from the church," Rex continued.

"Yeah. I've heard that too," I replied.

I had a bad feeling from when he first pulled in, but then I saw two more back-up cruisers come and heard his radio began to crackle with distorted voices. He reached down and unclipped his holster, then put his left hand on his taser.

"Mrs. Lynch said it's about half-a-million gone missing," he said, following it up with a whistle.

I read the writing on the wall. I put my hands on my head.

"Go ahead, Rex," I said. "Do what you got to do. But I had nothing to do with this. Maybe you should look at the Lynches."

"And maybe you should mind your own fucking business," he said.

He came at me quickly and I swung hard. One hit to the face that knocked him back. I saw him grab the taser and swing it toward me.

A click.

Then....nothing.

***

When I came to in the cruiser, I muttered some words to Rex, who was up front.

"You're gonna pay," I said.

"What was that?" he laughed. "I think you got it opposite, partner. You're the one who has got the half-million to return. Plus, you just assaulted a fellow officer."

"I'm being set up," I said.

His head was there but was still blurry through the barrier in the back seat. I was trying to put sentences together as I plotted my next move.

"Lawyer," I finally got out.

"Sure, sure, we'll get you an attorney. Let me guess. Your old drinking buddy, Attorney Allcock. What's he up to these days? AA?"

I slumped back in the seat exhausted. Tasers will fuck you up for a few hours. I was in pain, but I also wanted to sleep after that electrical charge ran through my body.

The cruiser pulled into the station lot. There were a couple of officers waiting and they looked in with disbelief

"Shit, Rex," said O'Neill. "Did you tase, Mike?"

"Resisting arrest and punching a cop will get you the taser, boys. He knew what was coming when he threw that punch," said Rex. "Lock this religious embezzler up."

O'Neill and a younger officer grabbed me by the arms and legs and dragged me out of the back of the cruiser. They finally got on either side and guided me into the station to be processed.

The Chief was waiting by the door and shook his head.

"Finn, I thought you were an upstanding, God-fearing Catholic boy. Where's the priest? And where's the money?" he barked.

"I don't know. That's why I was there," I said.

"You violated your suspension," he said. "You're in deep shit."

"I want my lawyer," I said. "Give me my call."

"In due time, Finn. Get him processed and in the cell. We'll let him call his attorney when that's done."

***

The problem with union representation is that sometimes your union rep has their own biased and personal feelings about you. Rex had taken over the rep position the previous year. I'd get no help from him...he was too conflicted, so I went straight to my attorney. Pete Allcock.

He came in the interrogation room with his briefcase, donning a new suit from Brooks Brothers and a red silk tie.

"Talk to me, Mikey," he said with a serious tone. "Embezzlement?"

I was still in a fog from the taser.

"What are you talking about?"

"The accusation is you stole $500K from the church. And that priest, Father McCartney is missing."

"His name is Father McKenzie. What do you mean, missing?" God, my brain is so addled.

"They can't find him. But he left a note at the rectory spelling it all out."

Allcock took out a photocopy of the note and slid it across the table.

"He says you put the money in this Bitcoin account. Your name and Social Security number are on it."

I couldn't believe what I was hearing. Father McKenzie stealing my information for his gain. It didn't add up. I knew that this somehow went back to Mrs. Lynch. I set the note back down.

"Listen, you got to check this Lynch family out. They live on Stanley Street. Something is off with them," I said.

"Like what?"

"Well, she set me up with the Chief. I was at the pub with the priest, and he confessed that he was stealing from the church. He is the one with this Bitcoin account. The Lynches...they were blackmailing him. I think they are a family of long-time grifters."

"Okay," said my attorney. "I'll check all this out. Meantime, we are trying to get you bailed out, but they are going keep you overnight until we can see the judge tomorrow."

I nodded. He got up and left me alone in the room. Where was Father McKenzie? Did he make a run for it? I doubted that. Something was amiss, to say the least.

***

The judge was Jerome Coogan. He was a family friend growing up and knew my dad very well. He had presided over many of the cases that my dad brought him as a cop. There were also drinking buddies at the local country club.

The prosecutor presented his argument about the charges, and I stood quietly. When it was his turn, Allcock did something quite unusual.

"Your Honor, I request a meeting with counsel in your chambers before the plea is filed and bail decided."

Coogan looked up. He hated any suggestion of special treatment brought into his courtroom but realized this was an unusual case and made an exception.

"Object, Your Honor," said the prosecutor. "You cannot give special treatment because the defendant is a police officer."

Coogan also hated loud-mouthed prosecutors.

"Attorney Humphrey, don't you ever tell me what I can and cannot do in my own courtroom or I will charge you with contempt," he barked

Humphrey sat back down quickly.

"Bailiff, take the defendant away. Counselors, my chamber now."

***

Allcock came in a few minutes later.

"Good news," he said. "Coogan is letting you out."

I nodded.

"Bail?" I asked.

"$500K," he said. "But it has been paid."

"By whom?"

"Anonymous donor," Allcock said.

"Is that legal?" I asked.

"Coogan allowed it. Guy came up to me in the hallway on the way to his chambers and handed me an envelope."

"Who was it?" I asked.

"I'm not sure, but he says he is a friend of yours," he said. "Let's get you out of here."

A guard came and opened the door, and I walked with my attorney out of the courthouse.

That's when the black SUV pulled up. A tall man in a black suit got out.

"Officer Finn?" he asked.

I looked at him and Allcock.

"Yeah?"

"My boss would like to speak with you," he said. "Please, get in."

"Who is your boss?"

"A friend who just paid your bail," he said. "He can help you with this case. Please."

He offered me entry into the back seat by opening the door. I hesitated.

"You may have heard that the Lynches are also missing?"

"No, I hadn't."

He saw I needed convincing.

"They stole two million from my boss two years ago in Santa Monica, and he wants your help to put these two away for good," he said.

I knew it. These Lynches were professional grifters. They set Father McKenzie up, as well as me.

"Can I bring my attorney?" I asked.

"No," he said. "My boss will share some very personal details with you. It's best you come along. You'll be safe."

I looked at Allcock.

"As your attorney, I advise you not to go," he said.

"Do you have a better solution?" I asked. His look said it all.

I got in and the bodyguard shut the door. We drove away to a destination unknown.

***

It was on this day that I met Harold J. Rothenberg and he shared his story about what Father McKenzie and the Lynches did to his family.

"We were one of the richest families in America," he said to me, sipping from his gin and tonic. "Until the Lynches robbed us of our fortune."

We were sitting on the back terrace of his Newport mansion. I had noticed the "For Sale" sign out front, on Bel Aire Avenue as we drove in the crushed stone driveway. It felt like I was arriving at Jay Gatsby's mansion.

"These people used Father McKenzie due to his dark secrets," he said. "They blackmailed him and stole from your affluent parish. And now, I will help you find them."

I nodded as a servant dressed in a white suit set down a cold draft beer in front of me. The weather was warm, and I studied the blue Atlantic in front of me. The white caps rose, and I thought about what dark secrets Father McKenzie had.

"So, the Lynches, they went where exactly?"

"I'm not quite sure, but my private investigator has some leads. He brought us your story, as he is dialed into the police network, and I knew that it was another one of their grifts. These are awful people. I want to clear your name, but also, I want you to help me get my money back. Not because I need it, but I because I believe that these people need to be imprisoned for life."

I took it all in, but I struggled with what I could do.

"I am a suspended cop," I said. "I don't know how much help I could be to you."

"Well, you know someone else involved in this grift. You know him very well," Mr. Rothenberg said.

"Who?"

"Rex Gamell."

I was sipping my cold beer and had to spit some out.

"Excuse me? Rex? What does he have to do with the Lynches?" I asked.

"He is in on the crime," said Mr. Rothenberg. "He set you up. Since your arrest, my P.I. has uncovered evidence that Gammel met with the Lynches at least twice." The servant came back with an envelope and handed it me. I opened it and saw photos of Rex with Mrs. Lynch from a surveillance camera feed.

"They met, and I believe he is tied to Father McKenzie's disappearance. His stake is half. He actually blackmailed the Lynches on this one," said Rothenberg.

I nodded and finished my beer. It felt good to be correct, but my head was swimming with ideas on how to resolve all of this.

"Take this evidence to your Chief and clear your name," said Rothenberg. "If he is not interested in pursuing the truth, perhaps you and I will have to do this on our own. My driver will take you home now."

***

The drive back from Newport took a little over an hour. I knew my moves, but I was worried about the Chief and his loyalty to Rex. And worried about how deep within the precinct this could possibly go. Could the Chief be somehow involved too? The SUV dropped me in front of the station. I walked in and headed down the hallway toward the Chief's office. When I passed the supply room, I saw O'Neill there. He looked up at me.

"O'Neill, I need a favor. You have to trust me on this one."

"Mike, you know I can't do anything for you," O'Neill began. "Chief will have my head."

"If I told you I was afraid of my welfare, would that change your mind?"

O'Neill shook his head in disbelief that he was going to help me."

"Alright, Mike. What do you need?"

***

After a couple of minutes, O'Neill had loyally given me what I needed. I thanked him and made my way down to the Chief's office.

"Finn, you're not supposed to be here," he said.

I threw the packet on his desk and closed the door.

"It was Rex," I said. "He and the Lynches set up the priest. They found out his crime and made him steal more for their own gain. They held his secrets over his head, things that took place in the past. He knew a lot about matters in the church if you know what I mean."

The Chief opened the packet and studied the evidence that Rothenberg had delivered. It was all there in black and white. He set it down.

"Where did you get these?" he asked. "And how do I know that you aren't doing this to bail yourself out."

"The shooting," I said.

The Chief looked at me, startled.

"What about it?"

"Rex owed the guy money. Gambling. He executed him in front of me. I covered for him. I took the blame for an arrest gone wrong," I said. "He's been nervous that I'd have this conversation with you for the past five years."

"How deep was he in?" he asked.

"That time was $100K. This time, I'm thinking double. He caught the Lynches grifting operation on McKenzie and shook them down for that money. McKenzie would never do this. He turned to me as a cry for help."

The Chief nodded.

"Where is McKenzie now?"

"Dead," I said.

"You found his body?" he asked.

"No," I said. "But I know what my old partner is capable of."

The Chief got up and tapped his holster.

"Let's go get him," he said.

***

The ride over to my wife's house seemed to take forever. I worried about Rex's response and thought about the non-issued weapons he had stocked in his place. I thought of my kids and, even though all the wrongs she had done to me, I thought of her. When we pulled up, Rex was mowing the lawn with his shirt off. The Chief picked up his radio receiver and called in.

"All available units, report to 239 South Colbourn Street," he said. "Potential confrontation with a fellow officer.

He looked at me.

"Stay here," he said. "I'm serious."

The Chief got out and approached Rex. He looked at me sitting in the passenger seat bitterly and walked toward the Chief, who was informing him of the situations. I saw the Chief unclip his holster. I watched Rex's hands. You must always watch a suspect's hands. He looked jumpy.

By the time I unlocked the car and got out, the Chief was knocked out and Rex had his gun.

"You fucked up, Mike," he said, pointing it at me. "You are always sniffing around where you don't belong. Your whole career. You swore you wouldn't tell. Now I'm going to destroy your world."

"You already did that, Rex," I barked back.

I heard the hammer click back. Vanessa opened the front door and came out on the front steps.

"Rex, what is this?" she said. "Why is the Chief on the ground?"

I looked at her.

"He did it, Vanessa. He killed the priest, and he is the one who stole the money with the Lynches. He's a degenerate gambler."

Two squad cars pulled up behind me with their lights on. O'Neill got out and drew his weapon from behind his car.

"What's going on, Rex?" he shouted.

"You swore, Mike. I always knew you would rat me out," Rex said. "Partners take secrets to the grave. Don't you know the code? We took an oath."

"Best thing you can do is put the gun down, Rex. No one else needs to die," I shouted at him.

Rex seemed to be reviewing his options. My ex-wife was sobbing and collapsed on the steps. I thought of my own options, then decided there was only one.

My first few steps were quick, but he saw what I was doing and fired. The bullet hit me in the center of the chest, perfect police shot at the center of the body mass. I kept running despite the searing pain. When I tackled him, his gun went flying.

I saw O'Neill sweep in and kneel on him while another officer pulled his arm back.

As I lay there on my ex-wife's lawn, I was grateful because O'Neill had been a loyal friend and illegally issued me a bulletproof vest that day.

The Briefcase

O mar was late again.

It was an unfortunate trait, one that plagued him through his school days back in his small village outside of Cairo. His parents and schoolteachers had always warned him that this habit would come back to haunt him one day.

He sprinted effortlessly down the escalator into Piccadilly Circus station, cursing the café owner's name. Mr. Gradgrind had made Omar close the café for the third time this week, knowing full well he had to make the last train back to his flat in Kilburn Park.

Fortunately, the tube station was just around the corner and completely abandoned. If he missed the last train, he'd be running home—again. Back in Egypt, he'd have to run home from school as fast as he could if he wanted to get some dinner. He had eight siblings—four brothers and four sisters, and they would devour whatever dinner his father had brought home. Maybe that's why he took the job in the café when he came to London: a guaranteed dinner every night.

His hamstrings screamed at him as he had been on his feet since early this morning, starting with his 6 AM morning long run through Hyde Park. Still, he flew down the steep escalator and saw the last train just pulling into the platform at Piccadilly. The sliding doors opened. His night would be quite different if he didn't get on this carriage. He leaned in toward the door just as the British voice announced, "Mind the gap." The sliding doors shut behind his sinewy frame as he collapsed, exhausted, into a seat. He felt relief: he had made it.

Omar looked over and noticed that there was only one other rider on his carriage. He caught his breath, smiled, and gave a wave, but the other passenger did not make eye contact with him. It was a man, dressed in a navy suit, shiny black shoes, and he was adorned with brown-rimmed glasses, the kind Omar had seen bankers or barristers wear. He concluded that he must be rich and important: an upper-class Londoner, most assuredly. Next to him, on another seat, was a brown leather briefcase. Omar looked at the man's pale face—he seemed nervous, shaken up by something. He thought to comfort him by making conversation.

"Just made the last train. I was running late."

The man's eyes darted toward him. They were wild-looking, resembling those of a cornered animal.

"I'm a waiter in Piccadilly," Omar continued. "My boss. He kept me late."

The man said nothing. He took out a handkerchief from his pocket and wiped his brow. He was sweating profusely now. He loosened his tie around his collar.

Omar felt foolish with his nervous small talk, so he stopped.

They rode in silence for six or seven minutes. Omar thought of how hard he worked at the café and how little money he had made tonight. He'd like to tell his boss to go to Hell, but he needed the job to stay in England, never mind money to send home. Arriving in London a decade ago, he had been recruited to play soccer for a university north of London. When he got injured while playing, he was able to negotiate his visa to stay to live and work, but also to continue taking classes. He was a year or two away from graduating with his degree in English and thought about teaching at a secondary school when he was done. In his rehab, he'd even started jogging a bit then worked out with a local track club in the city and got good enough to travel around Europe to race the mile.

The train began to slow, and the man across from him got up slowly, leaving his briefcase on the seat. Omar watched him walk toward the opening doors.

"Hey, mate. Your case. You've left it," he shouted.

But the man kept walking and ignored his calls.

"Sir, you left your case behind..." he called to him again as he stepped out of the sliding doors, without looking back.

Omar studied the briefcase. What was in it? Legal papers? Maybe the man was a barrister. Either way, he needed to get it back to him somehow.

Omar looked out at the Oxford Circus tube sign through the glass. He would have a long run home if he got off here; there were no other trains this late. Finally, he made his mind up in a split second.

"Mind the gap..." the voice called out in warning.

He jumped up and grabbed the briefcase, making it through the sliding doors in the nick of time. He turned and saw the man in the suit running up the escalator.

As he readied himself for the sprint, he thought of that hot summer night in Italy at a track in Rieti where he had followed an American runner through four laps and ran a 3:48 mile. Catching this man in the suit who forgot his briefcase would not be an issue. He put his head down and bolted up the steep escalator with the brown leather briefcase swinging from his hand. When he approached the top step, the man was running in front him.

"Hey! Mate! I said you've left your case!"

Omar's booming voice echoed off the historical buildings in the square. The man stopped and turned around and stared at him. In the evening light, his pale face had a troubled look.

"Give it to someone who can help. They don't care."

"Wait? Who are 'they'?" Omar asked.

In the distances, footsteps suddenly came from a different angle. Another man appeared. That's when Omar saw the gun.

He took cover behind an ivory statue of Winston Churchill. A gun shot came next, and he watched in horror as the man on the subway doubled over on the ground. The shooter fired twice more. Omar was sure the man was dead. He came out from his hiding spot and moved back toward the Tube entrance, stunned at what he just witnessed. Suddenly, the shooter turned and saw him.

"You," shouted the man. "Don't move. Metropolitan Police."

Instantly, Omar knew he was not a policeman: the police don't carry guns in London, they hadn't for some time. His youth around Cairo also taught him about very bad people...and he had met a few....and some of them claimed they were police. This man was one of those. He recalled the terrorists attacking a food tent in Covent Garden. There was no gun to stop them.

"Put the briefcase on the ground and there'll be no trouble," he said.

His accent was hard to decipher—German? Russian? It certainly wasn't British.

Suddenly, Omar saw the shooter begin sprinting toward him and he knew it was time to run again. He turned and bolted back down into the Tube station as shots rang out behind him, ricocheting off the walls. Within seconds, he was back down the the now-still escalator. He prayed they hadn't secured the entrance to the tunnel yet. There was little place to hide in an underground station, ironic he thought because these very tunnels had served as bomb shelters during the Blitzkrieg—a perfect place to hide. Omar made it back down to the tracks and looked back up the steep stairwell. The shooter was still coming. He tucked behind a girder and, for some reason—unclear even to Omar—tried to open the case. It seemed the combination had been set by the now dead man and it clicked open. Staring down, he saw the documents, a flash drive, and.... a gun. He took it out and set the case down, checking the cartridge—it was loaded with gold bullets. The shooter got closer and saw that he had a weapon.

"I don't want any trouble, sir," Omar yelled.

He pointed the gun at him from behind the girder. The man stopped and lowered his gun a bit.

"Listen, son. I am a Metropolitan Police Officer. Just give me The case and you can walk away," said the man.

"You killed him" Omar cried. "Why?"

He felt his hand shaking.

"He is a wanted criminal. Now I'm with the police, you understand. You're going to be in big trouble if you don't comply. Put down the...."

Without warning, the gun suddenly fired in Omar's hands. It was a single shot, and Omar was so shocked that he dropped the weapon and hit the platform hard.

When he looked up to see the man falling down the last ten feet of stairs. His body slammed against the cement. The blood flowed fast, puddling around him.

He panicked. Omar grabbed the gun off the ground and threw it back in the briefcase.

And then he ran.

***

As the sirens wailed in the distance., Omar jogged. He made it through. Holland Park and over to Paddington, then up the canal to Maida Vale, and eventually into his neighborhood of Kilburn Park in less than an hour.

It was quiet now.

He was sure that man with the foreign accent was not a Metro Police Officer. When he first came to London, he was stopped and searched by the Metro Police once while he was out on a run in Hyde Park—this man did not have that pedigree. The man was an imposter. A spy, perhaps? He had watched too many films in *The*

Bourne Identity series to realize that man wanted the briefcase, and he was going to kill him to get it.

He made his way down into his studio garden flat, unlocked the door, and turned on the lights. He set the briefcase on the table and stared at it.

"What have I done?" he whispered.

He knew they'd be looking for him. Cameras were all over London. The question was: Who would find him first? The bad guys or the police? As soon as they saw what happened, he would be accused of robbing and shooting a man. It was late now—past midnight—and he knew he had to get ahead of this situation. He opened his refrigerator and found a Fuller's London Pride, opened the can, and took a swig.

He was in this deep. This was Jason Bourne-identity level trouble.

He returned to the case and opened it. He took the Glock out and set it on the kitchen table and studied what was underneath.

Documents.

They were stamped "Classified" in the corners. This appeared to be government-level, top secret material.

"Oh God, help me," he whispered.

But then, a wave of greediness swept over him. In the delirium of the moment, Omar wondered to himself about their worth. Maybe he could sell them for a hefty sum, and he wouldn't have to answer to his boss anymore. However, he knew that man would be looking for this very soon. Stolen government documents.

Why did the stranger want to leave them on the Tube? Did he want Omar to take them? Did he know he was about get shot when he got off the train? So many questions and so few answers.

Underneath the documents he found something else: a flash drive. It was labeled "Important: Watch."

He located his laptop, booted it up, and stuck the flash drive in. Suddenly a video popped up. It was the dead man from the train. He began speaking:

"Hello. If you are watching this, I am dead. You and I most likely had some sort of interaction, and I gave you this briefcase and the documents inside. So hopefully you can find someone honest in Parliament or law enforcement, who will know what to do with them. Do not got to the police. I am unsure of MI5 as well. You must choose carefully because what I'm about to tell you about could kill you as well."

Omar sat down and watched the video intensely.

"My name is Dr. Sebastian Cram. I am a professor at Oxford University. I brought this briefcase with documents to a member of Parliament to show them the nuclear capabilities of the Iranian government. This is not only the concern of them refining plutonium in Tehran, but also a more portable weapon of mass destruction that will be used in a terrorist attack in London. Now, you may ask why I know all this. The truth is that I designed it."

Omar paused the video and thought to himself, if this Dr. Cram designed this device for the Iranians, how would he be able to get back to London. They'd just let him leave with the information? It made little sense.

He hit play again.

"Now, you may ask how I escaped my Iranian captors. Excellent question. The answer is that Sebastian Cram is not my true name. I was born Chaim Wasserman. I have worked as a Mossad agent for the Israeli government. My father was born in Israel but moved to London and married my mother, who was an Iranian. It was a forbidden and frowned-upon marriage due to their ethnicities and religions. However, I was able to use my darker complexion and British identity to infiltrate the Iranian Nuclear Research Program as I held an Iranian passport. Like any spy mission, I needed to gain trust and help build the first transportable nuclear device. However, I was pulled from my mission by my handlers due to the fact they thought I was compromised. I was brought back to Israel for an intelligence debrief. It was there I learned that one of my assistant researchers had still been able to successfully detonate the device in an underground bunker approximately two weeks ago, 150 miles south of Tehran."

Omar whistled. He paused the video. He was tired but intrigued. He thought about sleep, but this was too important.

"These documents explicitly state the where and when that this attack will take place. Unfortunately, my discreet contacts in the British government were uninterested in this information if you are watching this video. They wrote it off in the same way the Americans did with the 9/11 threats from Osama Bin Laden. My life has been threatened and I have been discredited as a conspiracy theorist by a prominent member of Parliament. This was my last effort to pass them on to you, a private citizen, who has no ties to my line of work. Perhaps, a politician or the media will believe you. Perhaps, you can put them in someone's hands who cares. I have been in hiding in London for months. But obviously my time has come to an end."

Omar found a piece of paper and scribbled down the date and time of the attack. He stuck it into his pants pocket, then shut the laptop. He needed to sleep but wondered if they'd come looking for him here. So many CCTVs in London, he'd surely be tracked. After five minutes of pacing, he knew who to call. He picked up his phone and dialed. There was no answer, so he left her a message; she was surely in the middle of working. Then, he threw on a black sweatshirt and dark jogging pants. He grabbed the laptop and threw it in his satchel, opened the door and was off.

***

One of the classiest hotels on the outskirts of Kilburn Park was the London Marriott Hotel Maida Vale. Omar's girlfriend, Mari, was a housekeeper there. He shook off his fatigues and called her, saying it was important. She met him at the service entrance, and they snuck back in.

"You're going to get me fired, man," she scolded.

"I'm sorry. I'm in trouble," he said.

"Come."

They took the service elevator up to the top floor. She opened a door and motioned for him to follow.

Omar could not believe his eyes.

"This," said Mari. "It is the Rain Man Suite."

Omar whistled.

"In the name of Tom Cruise! This is amazing!"

"You can stay here tonight, but you have to leave by 8 AM. My boss will be arriving from Paris tomorrow morning," she said. "But we can be together tonight."

Omar smiled and leaned in and kissed her. He thought of the laptop and took it out of the satchel. He told her the story, about the dead man at Oxford Circus, and the mysterious man who shot him. Finally, he showed her the video. Slowly, Mari sifted through the documents.

"You have to bring this to the police," Mari pleaded. "This is serious stuff. They will deport you. And me! Get rid of this. It is a curse, man."

He shook his head.

"The man on the video said the police could not be trusted. This could be worth millions to us. You know who might want to buy this?" Omar said.

"Are you delirious? They will put two bullets in your head for this information when they find you stole it. You think this is a jackpot,

Omar, but this is only certain death," she said. "Get rid of it now. Put it in the dumpster."

"You are being irrational. Overreacting. Give me a cigarette," Omar said.

"You are a runner. You don't smoke," Mari responded.

"I do when I'm stressed. Give them up."

Mari reached in the front pocket of her dress and handed him the Silk Cuts, then her lighter.

"This is a non-smoking room," she said.

"I'll be on the roof," he said. "Don't let that out of your sight."

Up on the roof, Omar lit the cigarette and studied Northwest London. The sky was clear enough that he could see back out toward Westminster, the London Eye, Big Ben, and Parliament glowing miles away. He looked down on Maida Vale and saw a small pub, Queens Arms below with some staff sitting outside, having a drink on their shift. He'd come here from Egypt to realize his dream. It was fervor in many ways—this strange epiphany he'd had when he saw London in a history book in high school. It suddenly made sense to him: England was where his dreams would come true.

He talked about London obsessively, to the point that he alienated himself from his family, friends, classmates, even some of his teachers. But there was one man, Mr. Pete Elliot, who coached him in track and encouraged him to pursue this dream. He worked hard in academics, especially English, and when the college soccer scholarship came, he left and did not look back.

Now this suitcase could be his lottery ticket. He would become famous in another way. He would stop this terrorist attack, but he could sell this information first to someone in the press, or perhaps the authorities. The tabloids might pay him a hefty sum, and Mari would not have to clean the soiled sheets of rich people anymore. He would not have to miss his train after busing tables all night long to the point his legs ached, so much so that he struggled to run the next day. He would be the king for once. Fortune would be his.

Omar finished the cigarette and made his way back down the stairs to the room. He opened it with the key card and called out to her.

"Mari," he said.

She didn't answer. He walked in and studied the empty living room. Perhaps she would feel romantic tonight in this luxury suite. But when he rounded the corner, and entered the bedroom, he saw the error in his judgment. Mari was lying slumped, her body twisted in a strange position.

"Stop fooling around," he laughed.

But she did not respond. He reached out and grabbed her arm. That's when he saw the bullet hole in her head and the blood on the sheets.

Omar sat down for a moment. He felt sick and dizzy. Their love was dead, and he had killed her with this briefcase. As he was taking it in, his shock faded as he noticed there was something missing.

The briefcase was gone.

***

Omar sprinted down the hallway toward the main elevator. Velocity came from his rage. He heard a bell ring and the doors close. 12th floor. He'd have to sprint. He found the stairs and made it to the lobby in what he imagined was no more than three minutes. When he ran by the main check-in desk, he saw a man in a long navy coat carrying the briefcase by his side.

"Hey!" he screamed. "Stop!"

The man turned for a moment, then reached into his coat and pulled out a Glock. He fired three times. Screams came from the staff and some lingering patrons at the hotel bar. Omar ducked down and felt for the gun in his jacket and pulled it out to return fire. The first shot was wide, but the second hit the man so hard in the arm that he was forced to drop the briefcase.

Omar made his move and sprinted at him as fast as he could. He grabbed the briefcase, then spun around through the revolving doors and was outside. He bolted into the darkness toward Abbey Road.

***

Captain Albert Jaggers was in pain again. His right hip was aching as he walked through MI5 Headquarters. He came upon what was known as "The Situation Desk" that had twenty-five different CCTV cameras, all covering various parts of London. A young agent was monitoring them and looked up.

"What's the news, lad?" Jaggers asked.

"We've had a couple of situations, Uncle Albert. An operative was gunned down by Piccadilly. Metro Police informed us, and we are investigating. Second situation down in Maida Vale at the Marriott. A man, who was spotted at the first shootings, apparently shot a man at the hotel. Briefcase was stolen. Here's the video played back."

Jaggers watched Omar point the gun and fire, then grab the suitcase and run.

"Who is the victim?"

"We're not sure yet, but he's foreign. Foreign as in Russian. Fingerprints came up with his identity on INTERPOL. Vladimir Dialvosky.

Jaggers nodded.

"Let me see footage from Piccadilly."

The agent played back the video of Omar shooting the man with the gun in the tunnel.

"Hmmmm... he looks familiar. You have an ID on him, lad?"

The young agent pulled up a file on his computer.

"Name is Omar Ahmhed."

"Wait. The runner?" asked Jaggers

"Says here he came to London in 2015 on an athletic scholarship. Injured. Now works at an Italian place at Piccadilly called Bellagio. No prior offences. We believe the weapon is stolen."

"Tell me about this briefcase," Jaggers inquired.

"We believe the man shot above ground is Dr. Sebastian Cram, AKA Chaim Wasserman. Former Mossad. He brought evidence to the government about an attack, and it has been ignored."

"Wait. He brought it to us?"

"No, he took it to Parliament. Charlie Martin, a member from Shipton Moyne."

"Why him?"

"Not sure, but Martin brushed him off and did not report anything to us."

Jaggers nodded.

"Bastard probably wants a terrorist attack to further his causes. Lock down the whole country, he would," he said. "Do we have eyes on this Omar fellow? If it's the same guy, he's run a 3:48 mile so he can run. Not a bad university footballer either. Before he was injured, Arsenal was looking at him."

"He was headed toward the canals," the young agent said.

"Grand," said Jaggers. "Get eyes in the sky. I'll head back to my old neighborhood too. Let's go!"

***

Omar sprinted down the canal toward Paddington with the briefcase in hand. If he could get to the station in time, he'd hide for a few hours, then get the first train in the morning and get the hell out of London. But where would he go? The canals were damp, and he slowed to avoid slipping and falling. He tucked into a corner of a bridge, then saw the helicopter hovering above, the flood light shining down. A voice came in the darkness.

"Omar. We know you are down there. Come out now. We want the briefcase. Please surrender."

His heart leapt. He should have known better than to pick this stupid briefcase up. Two people were dead because of him, and his love was gone forever. He looked at the canal and contemplated. They surely had those thermal trackers looking for his body heat, it was the only way they could have found him.

Jaggers came around the corner and saw him in the shadows. He clicked on his flashlight and smiled.

"Hello, Omar."

Omar held the gun out in front of him, pointing it in his direction.

"No need for that, lad. I'm a friend. My name is Jaggers," he said. "I used to hide from my father in this very spot when I was a boy."

Omar didn't trust his words.

"Lad, you've gotten into some trouble this evening, but I'm here to help. I need you to come into MI5 Headquarters with me."

"I was instructed not to trust you. Men have tried to kill me tonight. All I did was try to return this briefcase."

"We know, Omar and we are aware what's in it. I can help you because you are helping us stop the terrorists. Now, I could leave you here, but you know that man will find you and kill you like he did to your fiancée. Or you could come with me to the headquarters, and we could sort this out," Jaggers said, reassuring him. "None of this is your doing. And you can shake that delirious notion that what's in that briefcase is going to make you rich. That's never going to happen. You'll be dead before you hand it to someone who promises to pay you."

Omar weighed his options. Jaggers was right, even if he made it out of London, these people would not pay him. They would find him and kill him. He had seen *The Godfather* and he knew the fate of Jason Bourne. There was no escape.

He stood up and set the gun on the stone walkway of the canal and put his hands on his head.

"Good lad," said Jaggers.

***

Jaggers walked Omar down the hall toward a conference room with glass windows. Men were waiting for him at a large table.

"Now, Omar," he said. "These men are going to ask you some difficult questions, but this not an interrogation. We want to get all the details about you and how you acquired this case, then you and I can talk about where you want to go away for your own safety.

"What do you mean 'go away'?" Omar asked.

"I meant that MI5 has a relocation program to protect your identity. In other words, we can send you any place in the world due to your cooperation with our agency. This is with the condition of your complete silence. No one can know about this. We want to stop this terror ring before they kill people. Do you understand?"

Omar nodded.

"Well, here we go," said Jaggers. "Cheers and thank your cooperation."

He opened the door and let Omar in. It shut, and Jaggers stared at the questioning session through the glass. He knew Omar's fate. He'd be sent back to Egypt. The bastards had done it before to people who helped MI5. It was beyond his control. He thought of how fate brought Omar to that Tube station, that train, that particular carriage.

If only the poor lad had missed that Underground train.

Jaggers looked at his watch. It was time for a pint. Perhaps it would create a sense of delirium, an escape from his thankless job: intoxication to alleviate the chronic pain in his hip.

***

It was the following Saturday and Jaggers was sitting at the Queens Arms downing his third pint of Fuller's London Pride. Arsenal was playing Chelsea and he was lucky to retain his regular spot at the bar. He liked the taste of Fuller's a little too much and his GP had told him he'd better calm down with the drinking if he wanted to make it to retirement. He wasn't getting any younger.

Jaggers stood up and made his way through the crowded pub, out to the front sidewalk with his pint. The lads were all; gathered there in a circle, talking about girls, drinking, and smoking cigarettes. The sun gleamed down upon them. *Ah to be young!*

He bummed a Silk Cut off one of the lads and they lit it for him. Life was good. Retirement was closing in and he and the wife would head south to Portugal. He'd heard it compared to Florida in America—where all the old people go to die. Jaggers sucked in the smoke and savored it. His GP would not be pleased.

He thought of Omar and how word came back that he had been sent back to Egypt. Agents had milked him for all the information they could on the briefcase, anything he had read or memorized. He didn't know too much. Besides, no one would believe him.

After things quieted down, Jaggers had gone back to the evidence room and reviewed their bloody plan. It was a dirty nuclear bomb the Iranians wanted to set off—it would have taken out half of Westminster. He gulped down the last of his Fuller's and set the glass down on the brick wall. He would be sad to leave Maida Vale, but the real estate market was lucrative, and the wife had enough of London after all these years. He imagined himself on a sun-kissed beach in Portugal near Logos, Algarve. The sun beating down, the blue peaceful waters of the ocean and miles of honey-colored limestone cliffs.

So, when the sniper's bullet hit him in the temple, the imagery was still floating through his mind.

Jaggers slowly took the Silk Cut out his mouth, after one last inhale, and dropped it to the ground. He followed the cigarette to the pavement few seconds later.

Across the street, Gabriel Bradley unscrewed his favorite silencer and stuck it in his pocket. He broke the rifle down quickly and stuffed parts down the small chimney pipes atop of the London Marriott Maida Vale. He hated working with the Russians, but they paid well, and they'd told him that this agent was dirty, caught up with terrorists in a scheme to blow up London.

The narrative never mattered to Gabriel, just as long as the direct deposit went through to his account.

Back down the sidewalk, he passed the Queen Arms as police cars swarmed the pub. He observed Jaggers on the ground and snapped a quick photo with his phone and texted it to the Colonel back in Providence. Within ten seconds his phone rang.

"Hello?" he said.

"Nicely, Gabriel."

"Can I come home now?"

"Not quite yet," said The Colonel. "Have you ever been to Egypt?"

Police on My Back

The Internet screwed everything up; it always does.

This sentence spun around her head as she moved slowly through international customs at Heathrow, waiting to show her passport and declaration card. The failure to restrain herself from such a childish post made her feel like a fool.

She had caused this in a moment of delirium and vanity.

It was one stupid photo that she shared on Facebook. She was seventeen years old, and in love, and she wanted to show her circle of suburban moms how young and beautiful she had been.

How stupid! How vain!

She loosened the scarlet scarf around her neck—her breathing felt constricted. Then she unbuttoned her long, camelhair coat a bit. She just wanted to blend in with the tourists, just an American woman, away on business. British accents echoed off the walls that contained this diverse crowd arriving from Boston and other international destinations. Finally, she made it to the window and the immigration officer asked her the usual questions.

"Traveling for pleasure," she stated firmly.

"And where are you staying, madam?"

"West London. Maida Vale."

The officer grimaced. Perhaps he had discovered her identity, or it was just gas from his English breakfast. He studied her documents closer, as if it was clear they were fake. Setting them down, he typed something into his computer. He looked up at her quickly, then back down, then frowned.

"Just a moment, madam," he said as he rose from his cushioned stool.

She turned and observed a British police officer with an automatic weapon. She studied his freshly pressed white sleeves, and the unique cap caught her attention for some odd reason. She imagined his wife pressing it on her ironing board, smoking a cigarette with a cup of tea by her side. Then, he put it on and went to work and drove to Heathrow. Suddenly, there was Dermot with the gun to his head and he smiled at her. She heard the gunshot and saw the British soldier fall to the ground.

The vision came into her head so fast but—she did not know where it came from. She gasped, startled by her daydream nightmare.

"Madam," came a voice.

She turned back to the immigration officer nervously. He slid her passport back toward her.

"You are all set. Have a wonderful holiday," he said. "Next!"

She slowly reached down and took the passport. He deposited the travel card in a slot. She moved away from the window briskly toward baggage claim.

As she waited by the turnstile, she took out her burner phone that she had stored in her "go bag" and dialed the number. The buzzer sounded and a red light began to turn as she watched the bags slide down onto the black belt. A man with a sleepy British voice answered.

"Hello?"

"Good morning. This is Vodafone. Are you happy with your current cell phone carrier's calling plan?" she said as if she had been rehearsing the script for years.

"Where are you?" the man asked.

"Heathrow. Terminal 4."

"Right. I'll send a car," the man's voice said. "Be on the curb in twenty minutes. Exit past the Café Nero."

"Cheers," she said, hanging up the burner. She nonchalantly dumped it in the trashcan behind her.

She found her bag on the belt and walked through Terminal 4 briskly. The Clash played over the airport loudspeakers, and she sang along to an old song about the police being on her back.

She imagined her husband waking up back in a small Colonial they owned in a suburb outside Boston. He would reach over and find an empty mattress, realizing that she wasn't where she had been every morning for the last twenty years. They'd celebrated their twentieth anniversary at a nice upscale restaurant on Newbury Street just a few weeks prior. Their two children—a boy and a girl—would wonder why their breakfast wasn't ready and lunches packed. They wouldn't understand why she had had a "go bag" packed in their basement for the better part of their lives. They wouldn't understand how she had arrived at this critical moment, where she realized it was time to go—to disappear—for good.

And she threw it all away due to the temptation of the damn Internet, but she had thrown it all away thirty years prior. There was no changing the outcome, unfortunately.

She drove the car—that was her only crime. They chose her.

Things had turned violent in Belfast in early March of 1988. She was just finished with secondary school and had planned to go south to Trinity College in Dublin. Her parents wanted her away from The Troubles.

But she fell in love.

He was in the IRA and was considered a capo: his name was Dermot. She knew him in school as he was a year or two ahead of her at St. Columbkille's. His brother had been executed by a British soldier two years prior, and he was devoted to the mission to avenge his death and drive the British Army out of Northern Ireland. Her parents forbade involvement with anything to do with The Troubles.

But she was in love.

First, there was the death of three unarmed IRA members in Gibraltar, killed by British paramilitary officers. Then, a Loyalist attacked their funeral, shooting many attendees. She had been going to meetings with Dermot. She was trusted. Finally, she was given her orders to pick up two IRA officers on the edge of town. Dermot was one of them.

When she picked the men up on the edge of town, it was dark. As they drove, there wasn't much talking—these were soldiers on a mission, in a war. Dermot told her to relax and keep her eyes on the road and to stop and drive on command. If they were halted at a checkpoint, a high school girl driving would take off the suspicion. The dirt road was bumpy at times, but they made it out to the edge of town. At the first checkpoint, they asked her where she was going, and British soldiers came up to the car—there were three of them. She remembered that they were so young, like her.

Then it happened so fast. There were multiple shots from the back seat. It was over in less than ten seconds. She saw her identification card still in the young soldier's hands, him lying on the ground, and she looked at Dermot.

"Let me get it," she pleaded.

"Drive!" screamed the man in the back seat.

"He's got my identification," she cried

"Drive," said Dermot, putting his hand on her leg.

She drove. Her fate had been decided. Her identity left to fate.

When she returned to the safe house, they all went their separate ways. That was the last time she saw Dermot, and there was only enough time for a brief kiss and embrace before she was told to get in the trunk of an old Volvo and was driven over the border to the south. There was a safehouse in Dublin. But she didn't feel safe. After all, the British had her identification: it was the kiss of death for any IRA operative—her only hope was escape. She slept the night and walk to see the River Liffey. Half-Penny Bridge was in view. Members of the army put her on a ferry to Liverpool, where she drank a few Guinness and watched her face appear on the screen. She knew that she was going to be sent to America. It was the only sensible place to hide.

The only safe place for someone like her.

***

As the Uber drove, she watched the red brick-faced and white Victorian buildings go by through the window. London was a beautiful city: historical and romantic. Her parents had taken a trip here when she was in elementary school to see her father's aunt who had emigrated from Belfast. She was probably dead now.

She had struggled with depression for years following the shootings. It was easily sold to her husband as post-partum sadness—but it was rather occasionally catching her seventeen-year-old image at the post office on the FBI's "Most Wanted Terrorist" list. Her husband had encouraged her to seek professional help beyond her medications. However, she knew she'd be as good as dead if she did.

People with secrets they plan to keep to the grave don't go to therapists, she had told herself.

The car made its way into Maida Vale. It was such a classy part of West London. There were flowers and canals. They passed the Marriott, and the driver dropped her on a corner near Kilburn Park Station with a slip of paper and address on it.

120 Craik Court, London, NW6

"Go directly there," he said. "Don't stop or speak to anyone."

She got out walked up the street, and then through the Paddington Recreation Grounds. Runners were moving around the track in circles. She saw a fit Egyptian man running intervals and was taken aback by his physique and speed. There were new mothers pushing prams through the park. Her breath caught at that. She thought of her own children grappling with her mysterious absence. There would be tears and questions. The police would come and sit in their living room, interrogating her husband (they always suspected the husband). It was best that they knew nothing—there was no liability this way. Only the unknown.

They truly had no idea where she disappeared to...or why she disappeared.

Ultimately, the layers would be peeled back. The FBI would visit. She imagined her husband sitting down, holding his head, as an agent explained to him that an Irish emigrant had seen her on Facebook, tagged in a post entitled: Share Your Senior Year Yearbook Photos. And that that was the beginning of the end for her.

"Your wife was a member of the Irish Republican Army, sir," the agent would say bluntly. "She was involved in the brutal and heartless execution of three British Army officers in 1988."

She tried to fight off the guilt, what she had tied him up in without ever telling him. There was no other option: Delirium fades. Her fantasy life was over, but at the same time, she felt free, as if the boulder of burden had been lifted off her chest finally.

She made it to the other side of the park and exited onto Carlton Vale and found Craik Court just off it. She walked up the steps of the light brown brick building and rang the bell. The door opened, and she could not believe her eyes. There he was. Dermot, older and greyer, stood before her. He looked around as if to check that no one had followed her.

"Come in, dear," he said.

She followed him into the flat. It was nice, well-decorated, and she was impressed with his taste.

"Very nice," she remarked.

She set her bag down and smiled. He opened his arms and they embraced for a moment.

"We will find you a place of your own," he said. "My wife and kids—I have a family now, you understand?"

She nodded.

"Me too," she said.

His face now looked older and sadder. At everything that they'd lost. She could see the wrinkles on his forehead and beneath his eyes more clearly now. Dermot had a life—like she did—a long way from Belfast. A long way from 1988. He was hiding in London—in plain sight—the last place they would look for him.

"I'll make some tea," he said, moving into the kitchen and finding the silver kettle.

She nodded and sat down at the kitchen table. He prepared the kettle, filling it with water, and lighting the burner. He brought out the tea box, two mugs, and some milk and sugar.

"How have you been?" he asked. "It's been a few years."

"Grand. Been living in Massachusetts for the last thirty-three years. I have a family now—two kids."

"That's wonderful," he said, then paused. "I'm sorry—there was no other option for you to stay."

"It's grand. I knew this day would come," she said. "What do you do for work?"

"I'm teaching at the university now. Irish Studies, of all things."

The kettle whistled, startling her for a moment. Dermot went to the stove and brought it back, pouring the water in the cups. She opened the box of tea from Harrod's. She chose a breakfast blend as fatigue enveloped her. She'd taken the red eye as most do from Boston. She had only gotten the tip from her IRA handler yesterday after she had picked her children up at school. Dermot sat down and began to steep his tea bag in the steaming hot cup.

"So, they found you," he began.

"I was stupid. Someone must've recognized my photo on social media," she confessed.

"That's why I never opened a Facebook or any other social media account," he said. "I grew the beard upon arrival over here. Kilburn Park had many safehouses in those days. Then, I just integrated with my new identity. Total assimilation," he said.

She noticed; he had lost his Irish accent. It was more of a proper English now.

"So did someone approach you?" Dermot asked.

She nodded.

"Yeah. In a supermarket, of all places. She came up to me and said, 'I know who you are and you're gonna pay.' At first, I didn't comprehend it. Here I am in a supermarket in Massachusetts thirty-plus years later, and a woman from Ireland recognizes me?"

Dermot nodded.

"Boston has a ton of Irish. Did she get violent?"

She shook her head.

"She just held up her stupid phone. It was me at seventeen. I posted it on Facebook the week before, thinking nothing of it. It was dumb mistake. Second worst mistake of my life," she said. "I'm not a soldier now. I never was. I'm a mom. And a wife. Or at least I used to be."

Dermot nodded.

"We always have to be careful. Have you thought where you want to go from here? Europe, perhaps?"

"I thought you were going to help with that?"

Dermot laughed.

"There is no witness relocation program. We do what we can to help each other," he said. "I have money and passports. Liam can help you get safe passage, but you don't want to be recognized in London. This could be the heart of the beast. MI5 has you on some list."

He sipped his tea.

"Seems like you got out of America before the FBI got in touch with Interpol. Liam can get you into France, probably in some sort of compartment on a lorry, then the rest will be up to you."

She didn't know exactly where it came from, but she started

to cry. Maybe it was being reunited with Dermot, or the thought of her poor husband and two children whom she got caught up in this mess. They would know who she really was very soon. She wondered how much they would hate her, or if the FBI would take her husband into custody and lock him up as an accomplice. She cried for her lost life, and she cried for falling in love with Dermot. She cried for her now dead parents (word had come in the last few years of their passing) and two siblings whom she would never see again. She cried for the old woman she would be, living in a French or Italian village, withering away, plagued with guilt for the young British soldiers who died, and for those whose lives she destroyed by driving those murderers to their mission. Suddenly, she felt Dermot's embrace.

"I'm sorry," he said. "I never imagined I would do this to you. I was young and stupid and wanted to be a soldier. It was a senseless war that neither of us had any business being involved in."

She wiped her eyes and looked up at him. Then she kissed him as if they were young again. It was a passionate kiss that lasted for a minute or two, but then he pushed her back as they both heard the knock on the door.

"Go to the bedroom. Stay there until I call you," he commanded.

She moved quickly and slid under the bed and listened. There was only one other voice. Dermot invited him inside. There was some laughing and she heard dishes being put into the sink.

Then, the undeniable sound of a gunshot with a silencer on it. She'd watched enough movies to recognize that whipping sound. Footsteps came closer, and the intruder rummaged around the room. She held her breath. The footsteps moved away, then the sound of the front door closing was all she heard. She waited and waited. She must've waited an hour—but it felt like the thirty years she had been away. Finally, she slid out from underneath the bed and gently tip-toed back out to the kitchen. She knew what she was going to see before she saw it.

Dermot's eyes were still open, but the first bullet left a very distinct hole in his forehead. There was a small puddle of blood. She wanted to stop and clean it all up, so that his family did not have to see this carnage, but she knew if she didn't leave now, she could end up dead herself.

Instead, she grabbed her bag and went out through the back door into the garden.

On the run again...what her life boiled down to.

***

She didn't know why, but she stopped at a grocery and bought some cigarettes—Silk Cuts. The mean girls had smoked them in rebellion at St. Columbkille's. They thought they were tough and had picked on her. Lighting one, she thought about the fact that she had been one of the good Catholic girls—at least until that night, only to become part of a murder. She wondered what those so-called tough girls were up to now. Not that it mattered, after all, it was doubtful they were on the run like she was.

She'd taken one of Dermot's caps to cover her hair that was now pulled up underneath. She sat in the Paddington Recreation Grounds and smoked a few more as she considered her move. The new burner phone was dead. They'd be coming for her too—some sort of British Army retribution assassin, she was sure of it. If it was the London Metro Police or MI5, they'd have arrested him, not shot him with a silencer. It was a vigilante; it was war. And it was she who led them to Dermot. They'd gotten vengeance on one of the triggermen...besides, she was just the driver.

However, getaway drivers were just as guilty in the eyes of the law, especially if someone was murdered. There was the case of Katherine Ann Power. She'd read her story about five years after she arrived in Boston. She had been a twenty-one-year-old Brandeis student at the time when she was involved in a bank and armory robbery in 1970. She was one of five people involved, and a Boston police officer was shot in the back. All she did was drive the getaway car. All four accomplices were caught and served prison time, but she hid in plain sight in Oregon for almost twenty-three years until turning herself in.

Fractured existence.

She left Boston and was wept for...here she was derided and hunted like a savage.

When darkness began to fall, she made her way to the Carlton Vale Pub and found a table in a dark corner. The TV flashed Dermot's image, then hers.

It was only a matter of time.

She enjoyed a hearty English dinner and ordered a pint. As she was about to pay, she saw Liam walk in. He saw her and turned his head awkwardly and went to the men's toilet. She left the currency on the table and carried her bag toward the ladies' toilet. The pub was bustling. No one seemed to notice them. When she got there, Liam grabbed her arm and pulled her into the men's toilet, then locked the door.

"Are you absolutely suicidal?" he whispered to her. "They executed Dermot."

"I know. I was there," she said. "I thought they were coming for me. I did this to him. I led them there."

"No, you didn't," Liam said. "He did it to himself. The prick was working on his autobiography secretly, and someone at the university turned it over to the Metro Police. There must've been a leak because the Orange Order is hunting all of you. They've got their revenge soldiers and assassins involved."

She nodded. When British soldiers died, reparations needed to be made. Dermot was first. Now, her photo was flashing all over the television. They would find her.

"Now, listen, we have to move quickly," he said. "Take this burner phone. You are going to walk to the Maida Vale Tube stop, and you are to take the Bakerloo to Piccadilly Circus. When you get off there, you will go upstairs. A black cab will be waiting at the entrance to St. Pancras Station."

He handed her a ticket.

"This will get you to Paris on the Eurostar," he said. "Once you are there, you are free to go your own direction."

Liam reached in his pocket and took out a card.

"This is an untraceable and unlimited debit card. The money is in an account in Switzerland. Use what you need to get to your new destination—Italy or Germany—wherever you wish. This will be our last contact. If you waver from this plan, or expose yourself, they will kill you. Do you understand?"

She nodded and he put his finger up to his mouth as he exited the men's room and disappeared into the pub.

She thought for a moment about all the running she would be doing—for the rest of her life. She exited the restroom and looked around. The pub was packed now, and she made her way out the door with her suitcase. She stood for a moment and thought some more. It was going to be a long journey.

The Maida Vale Tube station glowed in the distance. She took a cigarette out and lit it, savoring it as if it was the last cigarette she would ever smoke as a free woman. She couldn't do anything about her family: she assumed the FBI might help them into a witness relocation program, or at least provide security. But she knew they wanted her, and they would get her, maybe not now, but in a year, perhaps, as she was sitting in a café in Florence, or perhaps in five years on a rocky beach in Nice.

She decided this was her only ticket out. She dropped the

cigarette on the sidewalk and crushed it.

Up ahead, as if it was an apparition, she was mesmerized by the glowing blue London Metro Police emergency light on the silver box, just outside the Maida Vale station. Delirious thoughts clouded her mind. She was not right.

Her finger moved toward it and pushed the button twice. Then, she sat down on a bench and waited for LMP to arrive.

Her conscious felt clearer. Like Katherine Ann Power, she would pay reparations for her sins as well as she could now.

The Pineapple Kid

They call me the Pineapple Kid.

I don't care much because those two-bit asses just need someone to pick on and bully, and I guess it's me this year. I'm short but I'm smart, and karma is a bitch—they'll get theirs someday. Maybe, just maybe, I'll be the one to give it to them.

You see, I got this name because I live in a motel on the south side of town off the interstate. Yeah—you guessed it—it's called the Pineapple Inn. It's a dump and it's dirty, but it's home. I don't got too much stuff because most of it got burned in the fire at my old house last December—and no, I don't want to talk about all that madness that happened around Christmas last year.

But what I will say is that my dear old alcoholic dad burnt the damn house down because he set the curtains on fire while smoking a goddamn cancer stick. He was selfish that way, always had to have his hot coffee and a cigarette before he went off to his miserable job at the factory. But at least I'm alive. Can't say that about my poor sister and mother. They never made it out. My dad hit the bottle even harder shortly after their deaths and, quite honestly, I don't know if he's gonna be alive much longer. That leaves me to fend for myself. And I don't want you to feel all sorry for me, like I'm one of those Charles Dickens's characters—Oliver Twist or Pip Pirrip types—but my life is hard; hell, I could sure use an anonymous benefactor, like that convict that supported Pip—hell, I'd even take Daddy Warbucks from that *Annie* movie at this point, if only to bail me out of this misery.

The truckers come in off 95 at night, park not too far from the Pineapple, and I hear them fucking the whores next door until the late hours. That's why I stole these wireless earbuds from some kid at school: to drown out the screams and moans. Believe me, when you're trying to get some shut eye, stealing those buds from a rich kid was worth the risk of getting suspended. Sometimes the whores and truckers even fight and smash lamps when they finish, and the manager, Reginald, will come down and throw their asses out. He's got a gun, I've seen it. He's a tall guy, and I think he must have played high school basketball because he's like six-five. Truckers won't fuck around with guns because they know most people who have them ain't afraid to use them. Still, some of them truckers, they got families, and one guy from South Carolina even threw me a few bucks when I told him my sob story. I ran into him having a few beers outside his room one night, and he just wanted someone to talk to. He said all those days in the truck cab, driving across America got lonely. He prays a lot and reads the Bible when he gets to a motel. I read it sometimes, too, but I don't know if I believe all that scripture stuff.

When my dad disappears and rent is coming up, I tend to have to steal and pull some cons to make money. I went a week without eating, and Reginald noticed and said if my dad didn't come back to feed me and pay rent, he threatened to call the police and the department of child social services. That would put me in the foster system...I've seen kids at school who are in that system, and they are trash. Not because I'm judging them, but they got stuck in some house they don't want to live in, with people who only want them around to collect a check each month, and you never know the intentions of some of these foster families. Usually, they are in it for the money, but other times it's for very different reasons.

So, I'll steal just enough and sell it to who I can on Facebook Marketplace or Craigslist or maybe one the truckers, then pay Reginald to shut him up for a month. He said it ain't personal, but his boss said if me and my dad don't pay, he was to kick us to the curb. Everybody's got bills to pay, but I got bills that no honest man can pay right now.

So, I gotta do what I gotta do.

When you are in this deep, left alone without even one person who cares whether you live or die, and every turn is a dead end, you start thinking about escape. I was reading some James Joyce recently. I got this English teacher, Mr. McCartney is his name, who thinks that his students can understand Joyce, an early 20th century Irish writer. He's delusional. He tells stories of backpacking through Ireland and France and staying in these hostels—hotels for the poor if you will—where you have to put your luggage in a barrel and lock it up every night. Tales of taking the train, Euro Rail, or something like that, all around Europe and shit. But there was one line in Joyce's book that I remember that stood out to me: *Delirium Ends*. It was in a story about a boarding house in Dublin where this older guy has an affair, gets the owner's daughter pregnant, and is forced to marry her. I took some Latin when I was a freshman—yeah, ain't I a veritable Pandora's Box of surprises—back when we had kind of a nicer house in a better part of town. I knew that delirium meant a serious disturbance in mental thinking which leads to confusion, disorientation, and distraction. It happens fast, and some folks have a reduced understanding of their environment.

Once, I got ahold of a record player and bought some cheap records. Buddy Holly's song "Not Fade Away" was one that caught my attention. I read something, where John Lennon said, "The only person you need to listen to was Buddy Holly." Those words struck me for some reason since John Lennon was in the Beatles and they are considered one of the best rock bands ever. So, what was it about Buddy Holly that made him so special?

Anyway, combining those two thought processes, I recalled Joyce and love fading away and I wrote down "Delirium Fades" in my notebook. And it does. Like when my house burnt down. Everything was pretty damn good with my family before that. Then I started thinking about when my dad gets drunk and when he sobers up. The good times are over...that psychological state of enjoyment—whether naturally or by way of liquid—when the dopamine is shooting through your brain, just dies.

Anyway, I took that *Dubliners* book by James Joyce up to Mr. McCartney and pointed out that line to him.

"This right here, the delirium. I think my dad has this," I said.

I know that Mr. McCartney kind of knew my story. He took off his glasses and smiled.

"Jake (that's my real name)," he began. "You think your dad is delusional? Do you think he has a condition? Like Alzheimer's?"

"Nah," I said. "What I think is that all human beings fall into this delirium crap. Like when they fall in love or get caught up in some fantasy. Or when they take drugs and drink. They get delirious with the feeling. They feel they can't live without it. It's like an escape mechanism."

Mr. McCartney beamed.

"My little Joycean scholar. Spot on. Well, done!" he said. "Where else did you see this in the book?"

And we got talking. I brought up the little kid who fell in love with his friend's older sister in *Araby,* not to mention that crazy priest in *The Sisters*. Every character in that book reminded me of myself because they felt all paralyzed—not literally—but stuck in their lives, and wanted to get the hell out of Dublin, Ireland, but ended up staying because it was like their fate or something. In the end, I kind of loved that book but I never admitted that to him.

Mr. McCartney was always giving me books to read. He was constantly telling us not to fall down that rabbit hole on the Internet, playing video games, or watching Netflix all the time. Next thing he gave me was *Ulysses,* this thick Bible of a book, almost as big as Stephen King's *The Stand*. I read half of it when I realized that James Joyce suffered from delirium too.

School was a goddamn escape for me. It was six hours out of my smelly-ass room at the Pineapple Inn. In many ways, I guess you could say that school was my delirium.

It was a typical Friday. I was pissed off because I was looking at two days back in the room. I was walking down Route 1 alone when I saw them coming on their bikes. I had a wad of cash in my pocket, plus some other stuff I stole from kids at school in my backpack.

"Hey, it's the Pineapple Kid! Watcha got in your backpack today, fucko?" laughed Tim Conroy.

He was a big, fat, punk-ass bully who regularly picked on me, going back to recreational basketball, where he broke my nose. I despised him even more because the coaches thought he was a terrific player and an all-around great guy. Truth was, he was an asshole.

"Nothing. Get out of here," I shot back.

"Heading back to the Pineapple Whorehouse Motel?" he quipped.

His goons, two kids who were equally as obese, cackled like hyenas behind him.

I tried to walk around them, but they moved their bikes to block my way.

"Let's see whatcha got in that backpack."

"No," I said.

Conroy nodded to one of his goons. I looked for an escape route, but I would have had to run out in traffic. I held onto the straps of my backpack and backed up.

"Get the fuck off me," I said as one kid grabbed my arms, and the other ripped off the backpack.

"Open it," commanded Conroy. "Check his pockets too."

The goons found all the shit I stole from the locker room, and I fought hard, but they stuck their hand in my pockets and took the cash that was supposed to go to rent this month.

"Well, lookie here. Gotta a couple hundred bucks, you are a filthy little thief. The Pineapple Kid is a little locker robber," said Conroy.

I was so angry, but I felt tears roll down my cheek. I broke free and pushed Conroy's bike over and he fell into the street. A truck came around the corner right at the exact moment and absolutely demolished it. He got up, angry now, and came back at me.

"Hold him," he screamed.

The goons grabbed my arms and held them behind me. Conroy head-butted my nose, and I felt the blood explode all over my face. Even the goons were shocked and let me go.

"What the fuck, Tim?" said one of the goons. "Why'd you have to do that?"

"Get his backpack and throw everything in there. He owes me for a bike anyway. Let's go before the cops show up."

I fell to the ground and went into the fetal position. I was messed up. My nose was broken. Blood was all over my hands and clothes. Cars sped by, and even a few assholes honked at me. No one stopped.

By the time I got back to the Pineapple Inn, the sun was setting, and I was equally as broke as I was when I left earlier that day.

Now, I'm going stop here and tell you that besides all this misfortune that had just occurred, something life-changing happened this very same day: I met Buck Green. As I was bleeding, I staggered past the other rooms, and Buck was sitting outside smoking a cigarette. He was coming through Massachusetts on his way out West with a rig of appliances. He stood up with an astonished look on his face.

"Jesus, my Lord and Savior," he said. "What in the hell happened to you, son?'

I stopped and, for a moment, I looked out at the empty blue hotel swimming pool and weeds growing on the burned-out lawn around it.

"I got jumped," I said. "Some kids from school robbed me and beat me up."

"Sons-of-bitches," he said.

Buck had a southern accent, like southwestern, I figured from Texas. He was tall and wore a white cowboy Stetson hat. As he smoked, he reminded me of The Marlboro Man or John Wayne in one of those black-and-white Westerns that came up on my TV each night. Buck squinted with these movie-star blue eyes that came from somewhere deep in his Scandinavian DNA, as his relatives came to America and rushed for land in the West.

"Let's get you cleaned up. Where's your room?"

I nodded over to the right.

"I'm fine," I said a little fearfully.

When you're a young kid who lives in a motel off the highway, you get a little weary of strange men. Everyone had the potential of being a predator. I learned really fast that truckers were usually after one of two things: your wallet or your ass. I'm fifteen, but I'm worldly smart. I didn't have any other choice. I knew my dear old dad wouldn't be here to protect me, and Reginald tended to stay away from conflict. I tried to look really aggravated at Buck, as if I didn't like him talking to me. I'd been watching a ton of those James Dean movies lately. He mastered this look.

"Listen, I gotta go," I said. "Real nice to meet you."

"Name's Buck....Buck Green."

His name sounded tough, brave—hopeful.

"What's your name, kid?" he asked.

"Jake," I said.

He stepped forward and I heard his black cowboy books click on the sidewalk. He wore crisp blue jeans that looked as if he pressed them. He stuck out his hand. For a handshake. With a teenager.

"Well, it's a pleasure to meet you, Jake," he said. "Please let me know if you need some help with those bullies."

That's when I saw the gun on his hip, underneath his jacket. I shook his hand and backed away toward my hotel room.

The truth is that me and Buck talked later that night, after I cleaned up and came outside and sat down in the lawn chair outside my room. I told him everything—about my deadbeat dad, my sister and mom dying in the fire. He sat and listened to my story and seemed to empathize with my pain. I was exhausted when I was done and got up and went to bed. I felt a little less alone in the world meeting Buck, but I still didn't know if I could trust him.

***

My dad never came home that night, and I started to wonder if he'd ever come back. I took a shower and tried to clean up my bloody face. My nose was busted, there was no getting around that fact. I was stuck here for two days on my own, and Conroy and his thugs stole my rent and meal money. Reginald would not be pleased.

I came out and laid down on the bed and fell asleep for a couple of hours. They tell you do not do that if you think you have a concussion, but I didn't give a shit. The adrenaline rush of being around Conroy and his goons had finally bottomed out and I needed to sleep.

I awoke to knocking on the door. Pounding, really.

Staggering up, I put on some clothes and looked through the peephole. It was Reginald. I opened it.

"Jake, the cops are here. They want to talk to you and your dad."

I panicked. Was it because of the shit I stole at school, the same stuff Conroy stole from me?

"Come with me up to the front," said Reginald.

I followed him slowly. I was scared. If they found out my dad was missing, not only would they arrest me for the stealing, but they'd probably throw me in some juvenile delinquent foster program. Either way, I was screwed.

That's when I passed Buck's room. Johnny Cash music was blasting through the door—I had heard it before...

But I shot a man in Reno

Just to watch him die

When I hear that whistle blowin'

I hang my head and cry....

I heard Buck singing along, and he let out a whoop and laugh like no other I had heard before, almost like a high-pitched hyena.

"Wait a second," I shouted to Reginald.

"What?"

"Look at me," I said. "I got robbed and beat up today, but them cops are going to take me away and throw me in a foster house 'cause I stole that shit, Reginald."

He looked at me and shook his head.

"Serves you right. I've been putting up with you and your deadbeat father for almost a year now. I want you out," he said.

I nodded. I was just about out of options. Then I decided I had to advocate for myself because Reginald wasn't going to. I jumped toward Buck's door and started pounding on it.

Reginald looked at me, astounded.

"What in the hell are you doing?"

"Creating some options," I said.

Buck opened the door. I could see he had been drinking, and there was a young lady sitting in his room.

"Well, there is my buddy, Jake!"

"Buck—I need your help," I said.

"What seems to be the problem?" he asked.

He came outside and looked at me, then Reginald.

"This guy giving you a problem?" Buck asked.

Reginald was taken aback.

"The cops are here for me," I said. "They are going to take me away."

Buck looked at Reginald.

"Just because your daddy is gone? he asked. "And what are you doing to help this poor kid, Mr. Reginald?"

"And I'll admit, I stole some stuff at school," I said. "But those goons who broke my nose took all of it."

Buck nodded and looked back at his female companion.

"Sit tight, sweetheart. I'll be back," said Buck, winking at her.

Reginald was flabbergasted. The walk from the rooms up to the front office was a long one. Buck put his arm around me and tried to reassure me.

"We are going to take care of this right now," promised Buck.

Reginald delivered us to two police officers, both looked at me, then Buck. Reginald cowered away to his back room to avoid further conflict—same as always.

"Jake Barnes?" said a tall officer.

"Yeah. That's me."

"This your father?"

Buck stepped forward and extended his hand

"Uncle."

The cops looked at each other, confused. One took out a small notebook.

"What's your name, sir?"

"Buck."

"Uncle Buck," laughed one of the officers. "Wasn't that a John Candy film?"

"Yeah, directed by John Hughes. *The Breakfast Club* guy," said the other.

"And *Home Alone, Ferris Bueller's Day Off,* and *Pretty in Pink,*" I chimed in.

"Those were good ones," said the tall cop.

Buck was having none of this conversation.

"You see, this boy's house burnt down, and he lost his mom and sister," Buck continued. "They've been renting here for a bit. I come up from Tennessee to apply to be the boy's guardian. My sister, may she rest in peace, died in the fire."

"Sorry for your loss," said the officer. "But your nephew here has been involved in some larceny."

"Right," said Buck. "Take a look at the boy's face."

The cops looked at my broken nose.

"He was jumped, robbed, and beaten today by three young men. What was that bully's name?"

"Tim Conroy."

The cops nodded.

"Yes," said the cop. "He is the one who filed this police report. He reported the stolen goods."

"Right. Now, I have to confirm with Jake here, but do you have a list of what was stolen?"

One of the cops handed him the report. Buck handed it to me. The $240 in cash was missing, as well as my backpack.

"Cash and backpack are missing," I said to Buck.

Buck took the sheet and stared at the cops.

"This kid is trying to cope with the loss of his mother and sister. and he gets robbed and beat up by these juvenile delinquents, and you have the nerve to come over here and harass him?" asked Buck.

The cops look astounded. Reginald, who was now behind the desk passively eavesdropping, tried to intervene.

"His father has been gone and they haven't paid their rent in...."

"You best shut the fuck up and mind your own business, Reggie ol' boy," Buck yelled across the room at him.

Reginald cowered back behind the desk, then walked into the back alcove.

"Mr. Green. We appreciate your concern, but this kid is going to be booked on larceny charges. And may I see some ID, by the way?" said one of the cops.

"What's your supervisor's name?" said Buck, taking out his cell phone.

The cop looked confused.

"Phone number too?"

"What—why?" said the cop.

"I'm going to let him know how you come over to this here motel and harass low-income residents, all the while ignoring the crimes of the more white-laced citizens of this here town.

The tall cop looked at the other one.

"Sir?"

"If you don't have a warrant, and you accusing a boy of stealing items that he has no possession of that you were aware, then this is hearsay. I'd like your supervisor's number and tell him that the Keystone Cops are down here harassing honest, God-fearing citizens. Did you even investigate this thug, Tim Conroy? Did you even look at the security cameras from local businesses around where this boy was beaten? Seems like this investigation is rather one-sided. Makes me want to call my attorney," Buck said.

The cops stepped outside and conferred. Buck looked at me.

"You have any contraband in your room?" he asked.

"No, it was all in my backpack. They took it every bit of it," I said.

"Good," whispered Buck.

The cops came back in.

"We called the station, and they are reviewing that footage now. Mr. Green, it seems that there was more to the story."

Buck beamed.

"Now, can this young man go back to his room and get some shut eye, and we can revisit this tomorrow? Like I said, I believe we need to consult our attorneys," said Buck.

The cops nodded.

"Yeah, go ahead," one finally said.

Buck looked at them.

"And where does he file the assault report, exactly?"

The young cop spoke.

"Just come down to the station."

"Well, that's swell," said Buck. "Thank you for your time, officers."

They walked out; a bit bewildered by Buck Green. Honestly, so was I. We watched them drive away in silence.

***

The next morning, I got a knock on my door. It was Reginald. I opened it.

"What do you want? My rent money?" I asked.

Reginal had a weird look on his face.

"What is it?" I asked. "What do you want?"

He began to speak, but his words were all jumbled. Then, he did this weird thing and started to cry.

"Reginald, what's wrong," I asked

"Your dad...he died last night," he got out. "The police want you to identify his body. They are on the way over."

I walked up to the front, past Buck Green's door. He was sleeping, probably, and I was in shock. I went with the cops in the car over to the hospital. They took me down in the basement to the morgue. A doctor led me over to a gurney with a sheet draped over it and pulled it up. It was my dad. He looked pale and stiff.

"The cause of death was a heart attack, but also cirrhosis of the liver," a doctor said to me.

I turned and walked out of the room. A social worker was waiting for me. We talked for a bit, and I told her I wanted to go back to the Pineapple Inn to get my stuff. Surprisingly, the cops took me back. They said they would be back in the morning to take me to foster care. Reginald had agreed to supervise me while I packed.

I felt numb. It was official. Every member of my family was dead. I was alone in this world, and I had to figure out where I was going to go next.

***

I walked over and sat in Buck's room and watched a documentary on TV. It was about the old-time rock and rollers.

"I'm sorry for your loss. Sorry I never met your daddy," said Buck. "I would have liked to talk to him."

"This was the longest he's been gone. Ever. I should have known he was dead," I said.

Chuck Berry did a duck walk across the screen, and Buck handed me a Coke and a bag of chips from the vending machine.

"You ever been to Texas, kid?"

I shook my head.

"Nope. Never left this here town," I said. "I'll probably die here, too, with my luck."

"Jesus," said Buck, cracking a Budweiser. "What kind of life view is that? You're only what?"

"Sixteen.

He finished his beer, then cracked another one.

"How about you come down to Texas with me, partner?" asked Buck. "I got a big ranch, forty acres or so, and I could put you to work down there. Teach you a few things."

I looked at Buck and laughed.

"Nah," I said. "I can fend for myself. I'll finish high school and live with some foster family. It will suck, but I'll be free at eighteen."

I got a real weird, nervous feeling, and I began to fidget a bit. Like I said, these truckers can get a little bit shady sometimes. At the same time, he had already stood up for me to Reginald and the police, so part of me knew he wasn't a complete scoundrel. But that didn't mean he didn't have an ulterior motive. I got up and sipped my Coke, then pulled the curtains back by the window and studied the Pineapple Inn sign glowing in the dark as the cars sped by on the state highway. My broken bicycle lay on the grass out front, and the security lights shined down into the empty blue pool with the busted diving board and cracked slide. A couple of whores were taking a break and smoking cigarettes out front, dressed in tight leather dresses, and high heels. The rattling of the wheels of a stolen shopping cart came and passed in front of my view, pushed by one of my Hispanic neighbors, José, with what appeared to be a stolen stereo system in it.

I let the curtain fall back and looked at Buck. He was playing the air guitar to Buddy Holly and the Crickets on TV as they sang, "That'll be the day when I die."

"I'll go," I said to him.

He froze, then smiled, and let out the loudest whoop I'd ever heard.

"Well, that's genuinely great news, partner," he shouted.

"But we have to do one last thing before I go," I said.

Buck took out a Marlboro Red and lit one. The smoke enveloped his figure.

"What'll it be, partner?"

***

We spotted him on his bike on the way to school. He looked kind of pathetic: big, fat, and sleepy, riding his now repaired BMX bike to high school down the secluded roads, out by the farms. No one was around. Buck drove his truck toward Tim Conroy and laid on the horn. He came close but did not hit him, and we watched as his front wheel hit the curb and he went flying into the iron fence.

"This is gonna be fun," said Buck. "A real hoot."

We jumped out and Conroy was on the sidewalk bleeding. He was hurt, just enough for him to be crying a little.

Buck's cowboy boots clicked on asphalt as he walked up and drew his Magnum. He pointed it down at Conroy.

"Well, what do we have here? A little bully picking on kids smaller than him? Yes, indeed," Buck said.

"You almost hit me with your truck. I'll sue you," Conroy said.

"Can't sue nobody when you're dead," said Buck, clicking back the chamber. "Believe you owe my friend Jake here some cold, hard cash and other items, Timmy-boy."

I stared down at his pathetic, bully ass. Buck looked at me, then handed me the gun.

"Go ahead, Jake," he said firmly. "Put this coward bully out of his misery."

The gun felt heavy in my hand. I held it up and pointed.

"Pull back the chamber," Buck said.

I pulled it back as if commanded by the devil himself. My right finger tickled the trigger.

"Pull it when you're ready," Buck said softly. "Do it."

I felt all the rage and embarrassment that Tim Conroy had caused me over the years. I would love to have been bigger and stronger and teach him a lesson with my fists, with each punch representing every ounce of the emotional pain he had caused me. I steadied the gun as my hand shook.

Then, as if by divine intervention, I saw him piss himself. His blue jeans darkened with urine. He feared my feral and primal metamorphosis. He saw death in front of him, and perhaps all his sins of bullying weak, younger kids were staring back at him.

"Don't, Jake," he pleaded. "Please don't."

I hesitated, which is never a wise decision with a gun. As I turned to hand the gun back to Buck, Conroy leapt up, and, by accident, my finger must've hit the trigger. The bang was so loud that I was deaf for a moment.

"Shit, partner. I didn't think I left any rounds in there," Buck shouted. "We got to get out of here."

I looked down and he was dead. I was sure if it. The bullet went through one of his eyes and blood poured out.

"Let's go!" Buck shouted, running toward the truck.

***

We were on the New Jersey Turnpike in the wee-wee hours when the radio report came out about the shooting. Buck turned it up and handed me a Marlboro Red. We smoked in silence as the announcer told the facts and put out the bulletin.

Somewhere around Newark, Buck pulled off the road and made a phone call. I fell asleep, and when he woke me up, I noticed we were at the airport.

"Partner, we got to separate. The police are going to track us down if we stay together, and it's too dangerous. I got this friend down here. He's in the disappearing business. You understand?"

I shook my head "no." He ignored that and popped the glove box.

"While you were out for a couple of hours, I made a stop, took the liberty of borrowing your wallet and license." He pulled out a passport and my new driver's license.

"Now, here is some cash. There's $1500 in there. I want you to go in there and look real close at the departure screen. I want you to pick a place to fly away and escape to," said Buck.

"Is he dead?" I asked Buck. "Did I kill him?"

"Nope. You wounded him really good, though," he said. "Probably never see out of that eye again, at least according to my sources. Eye for an eye, as I see it. He caused you a whole bunch of pain your whole life. Betcha he never picks on a kid again with his eye patch on. Maybe they'll make fun of him. Karma and all."

I nodded and took his gifts. I got out of the cab and Buck Green leaned out.

"Take care of yourself, Jake. The world is your oyster. Head on over to Ireland or England. I remember when we talked that first night you said you liked those Charles Dickens and James Joyce fellas," he said.

He revved the engine of his truck cab and laid on the horn. I watched Buck Green drive away that night and walked into to the terminal to buy a plane ticket. It felt good to leave the Pineapple Kid behind.

The Con

When Mary arrived at LAX on the red eye from Boston, she found a payphone and tried the number of the Hollywood talent scout, but it was disconnected.

She slowly walked out to the curb, set her suitcase down, and began to cry.

There was no money left—she should have taken everything in that envelope.

Then, without warning, a handsome man dressed in a gray suit tapped her on the shoulder. She wiped her tears away and turned slowly. In the California morning sun, he looked like a knight donning shining armor as he held out the silver cigarette case.

She took one, pressing it against her lips, and he swiftly lit it with his silver lighter.

"Now, what seems to be the trouble, dear?" he asked.

His voice was full of kindness. Mary smiled and looked down at his trumpet case next to his bag.

"Are you a musician?" she asked.

"Why, yes," he said. "My name is Chet."

He flashed his perfect white teeth as he hailed a yellow cab.

"Say, let's share," he said, reaching for her bag. "Where are you headed?"

She was speechless but she allowed him to take her bag carrying everything she had to her name. He set it down with his own baggage in the trunk.

"Santa Monica," she said.

"Nonsense," he said. "Come with me. I'm out in The Valley. Have you heard of the San Fernando Valley? It's much nicer out there."

She thought about her options. There weren't many. She could handle herself with this strange fellow for now. She'd figure out the rest later. Chet was her first step toward survival. There was no going back to Boston.

"Ready?" he asked, reaching for her hand.

She took it as he opened the door for her and let go to motion her inside.

This was in 1959. Mary was just eighteen years old.

***

The pink magnolia leaves were blooming, juxtaposed with the palm trees on Ventura Boulevard. They were the only pastoral element of nature around all this cement jungle called The Valley. The colors caught her eye as she spoke into the telephone.

"Yes, ma'am, you can send your donation to the Los Angeles Children's Literacy Fund to Post Office Box 2756, Studio City, California 91604," Mary said into the receiver with an Irish accent. "Bless your heart."

She lit another cigarette and blew a cloud toward the open window. The smoke collided with the smell of the pink magnolias. Her hair was gray now, and wrinkles were visible on her tired face. She looked much older than her fifty-eight years. Her memory was not so sharp anymore—she was forgetting where she hid things lately. Chet had left her in 1966—forty-three years ago—to go on the road with his trumpet and never came back...at least that's what the one and only postcard she'd received from Nashville implied. It was his last farewell.

"And one last thing, ma'am. Could you make the check out to Mary Peters and just put 'donation' in the memo? I can take care of the rest went it arrives."

She studied her desk. There were fake IDs scattered next to her bogus business cards. She was in the process of creating a fake passport with the local print shop owner if she ever needed to leave the country and go on the lam.

There came the usual momentary hesitation from the caller on the other end; there were always people trying to scam in Los Angeles, but Mary's voice always provided the reassurance and trust that her mark always fell for. Truth be told, there weren't many cons that failed for her.

"Yes. That's right, I manage the charitable fund. It's just for the purpose of tax filing. The State of California always wants to steal a little tax from the children, this way the kids get all the money you so graciously are donating. Yes. Thank you."

She hung up the receiver and looked back out at the pink magnolias. The combination of nature and concrete that surrounded her rent-controlled, one-bedroom apartment was astonishing. Orange orchards had once lined this boulevard, but that was all gone now. The farmers lost their water—anyone who had watched *Chinatown* knew that version of that story. The government wouldn't let the farmers purchase their irrigation supply, and it was no coincidence that farmland wasn't taxed the way all this million-dollar property was.

She was a cash, diamond, and gold lady. Mary Murphy from Boston didn't exist anymore: she had died that day at LAX. Instead, she was a variety of identities and personalities, all scattered out on documents in front of her. The best thing, though...none of her aliases had paid a dime in California taxes.

Mary thought about all she had survived in the last forty years: the Manson murders, protests, the Watts riots, the L.A. riots, never mind the Northridge earthquake. She had endured it all and made a fortune grifting, swindling, and defrauding folks.

Her dead father would've been so proud.

When she and Chet rented this place, the developers were still building homes across The Valley and she recalled the hundreds of frames spread across from Burbank to Sherman Oaks, then up into the hills near Mulholland. Chet had promised one for her and Liam. It was a simpler time: Chet was loving back then, but then as The Valley became more adulterated, so did he. He had slowly begun to drift away from her. Late nights at the clubs, numbers of strange women on matchbooks, phone calls where no one replied on the other end and abruptly hung up.

Finally, he had left her. The delirium passes, fading slowly. She recalled the words that Joyce once wrote. She'd read that line in "The Boarding House" in *Dubliners*, a book her father kept on their bookshelf in the family room in Boston. She now found her place in life was no different than Mrs. Mooney's. Her husband had gone to the devil, and she'd have to reinvent herself and deal with this setback like a cleaver deals with meat.

She poured a second cup of coffee and considered taking a walk up to Du-Par's for breakfast and the morning paper. Bacon and eggs sounded good to her now. The waitresses knew her well there: she was a good tipper and a regular customer. She'd even worked some shifts there before opting for a more lucrative job of lifting some customers wallets and checkbooks.

No one would believe that she cleared almost $50,000 a year pulling these phone sale schemes. Tax-free money that she discreetly put away in her coffers to survive.

Fortunately, she'd secured this now rent-controlled apartment on Ventura Boulevard and lived here ever since. She couldn't go back to Boston—most of her family were all dead now anyway. She did wonder what happened to her sister, Siobhan, how her life had turned out. Mary had ended all communication, which is what one does when they come to Hollywood. In many ways, the Mary Murphy from Dorchester no longer existed. She had reinvented herself here and made a living, in many ways, no different than those who drove up to Burbank Studios to act. There was no leaving this island she'd put herself on—it was for forever—at least in her mind.

Her mind was wandering more and more these days and she had started to forget things. She had gone to a local doctor, and he had run some tests. When the results had come back, she was not surprised: symptoms of early onset Alzheimer's. It ran in her family. Her mother had begun to forget things before she left Boston. Mary looked at the calendar in front of her and her cursive notes about her various scams and cons. A yellow phone book was open, and she studied the checkmarks of all the suckers she'd fooled into sending her money.

She smiled, then thought about her son Liam coming to visit her. He was always worried about her, especially now that she was forgetting things. She had raised him on her own and put him through college, all financed by her con jobs. She had led him to believe that she was a screenwriter, then later an agent—she had sold those lies to her son as easily as her cons. You could be both of those professions with few questioning the legitimacy of it all since everyone was acting in L.A., especially those who were truly in the film industry. She had modeled her card after that "agent" she had met in Boston, the one she'd tried to call when she first arrived in Los Angeles. In fact, she had become quite good at forgery and imitation over the years.

Men were few and far between. She did have a brief affair with the local printer, Mr. Sackostein, on the corner of Ventura and Laurel Canyon, but all they had now was a business relationship. She had convinced and compensated him to print her fake business cards, and then after hours, he would work on laminating her IDs. She was probably one of the lower-level criminals he worked with, but he loved her so much that he would print just about anything for Mary.

It had led to more and more money coming in, so she had invested in her own business card machine, as well as a laminator. Mary turned and studied the bookcase filled with blue-bonded cardboard scripts; the ones held together with gold-colored clips.

She must've written hundred over the years. She'd taken a class with Syd Field over at USC after attending one of his two-day seminars. In between class, she'd sold fake USC-Berkley tickets to undergrads, wearing her traditional redheaded wig, glasses, and stolen USC staff shirt. However, she always knew when to stop when the authorities were getting close. She kept most of her cash stashed under the floorboard in the bedroom. She wrote herself vague notes, hints for herself if she forgot where the money was, but even still, she was misplacing those now.

The life of a grifter, however, is never an easy one. Constantly looking over your shoulder, always working ten steps ahead of your next target. It's never ending.

And she was almost caught—one time—ten years ago.

One morning, about a decade before, her phone rang. She stared at it oddly. Her phone number was unlisted—only her son knew it. She was annoyed at first, but then felt panicked. Had one of her victims traced her number? She thought about it and then picked it up.

"Hello?" she said in a deep British accent.

No one replied.

"Hello?" she repeated.

She heard someone breathing.

"What are you? Some kind of perverted prank caller?" Mary asked.

"I know what you're doing," said a man's voice. "And it needs to stop. Today.

"Who is this?"

"You've been warned," he said. "I want $15,000, or I'll turn you in."

Mary slammed down the receiver. Panic ran through her body. Her mind raced: Was it the police? No. They'd just come and arrest her, not try to bribe her. Someone was watching her. She pulled her curtains closed and ran around the apartment trying to reduce her visibility. Was the phone tapped? Nothing had happened like this in thirty years of her cons.

She told herself to calm down and found her Camels, lighting one. Her inner voice was the friend who always reasoned with her. Someone knew what she was doing, but they weren't ready to stop her.

This was a shakedown.

Mary considered the suspects: Sackostein knew most of her secrets but was in love with her—plus, she knew all his wrongdoings. It couldn't be him. Then, there was the case of the retired police officer across the hall, Mr. Wasserman, but he never bothered her; and her son Liam was too busy with his law practice and would never harm her.

Then, it occurred to her...it must be someone like her, another grifter.

She was being conned now.

Mary had learned a few things over the years about the telephone and how it worked so she installed a tracking device and a recorder. A guy out in Reseda sold it to her for $40. She set it up and waited. The next call came the following Tuesday afternoon. She picked it up and held it to her ear.

"I said stop. You didn't listen," the voice said. "Now, I want you to meet me with everything you got. I want it all, or I go to the cops. All of it, and I know what's up there...every penny, diamond, and bar of gold."

Mary watched the second hand on her clock tick. She needed a minute to trace the call, so she had to slow things down and keep him on the line.

"I know who you are, Mary Murphy from Boston. Your days of grifting are all over."

The clock hit sixty seconds and she smiled.

"I'll see you very soon," she said into the receiver and hung up.

The trace went back to a payphone on Ventura by the Book Star bookshop. She walked down and scoped out the location. She had to do this on her own because this grifter probably didn't like her cutting into his operation. She found a coffee shop across Ventura and sat and waited. It took a week, but he finally showed. Her plan was well thought out, and she had to scare him away, but also make him fearful enough not to share her secret. She looked in her handbag. It was a handgun that she had stolen out of a house in Laurel Canyon when she had posed as a maid during one of her cons. She finished her coffee and walked across Ventura.

The man was probably in his fifties: argyle jacket, jeans, sunglasses, and a Dodgers cap. She came up behind him as he picked up the phone and dialed a number. She pressed the gun up against his back.

"Calling Mary Murphy from Boston again?"

The man froze.

"Don't move. It's loaded and I have a silencer on it, so when the cops find you, they'll have no idea who shot you," she stated firmly.

He complied.

"Now, who are you?"

"No one," said the man.

"You look like someone. Name?"

"I'm just trying to make a living."

"By blackmailing an old lady?"

"You're not old."

"Flattery won't work, buster," she said, disappointed with her word choice.

"What's your address?"

"Why?"

"We're getting a cab there and you are paying me off for all these harassing phone calls. Fifteen thousand sounds like a good number,

"Mary said. "Then, you will pack a bag. You're done in The Valley. This is my territory. Hear me?"

The man nodded, then slowly hung the receiver back up. She looked around but didn't see a single cab on Ventura Boulevard. Figures.

Suddenly, the man pushed her back and ran. Mary froze. She couldn't shoot him in broad daylight. She watched as he ran out into traffic, and then in horror as a cab flew out of nowhere and slammed into him.

Traffic stopped, and Mary ran out to the lifeless man on the street. She reached in his jacket as if checking for an injury and found his wallet and stuck it in her bag.

"Call an ambulance. Somebody!" she screamed as the crowd gathered.

Then, she got up and backed into the mob of people and disappeared.

Just what she did best.

***

It was late Saturday morning and she recalled that Liam would be there soon, pulling his BMW up to the curb and honking twice. He'd want to take her to someplace nice over in Santa Monica or Brentwood. He was successful now; she had cash-flowed his education with some bigger schemes along the way.

It occurred to her that she could reveal her game to him now that her diagnosis was in. Would he even care? She had to survive— an unmarried girl with an infant—living in The Valley, alone and jobless. There was no unemployment to be collected—she was invisible in Los Angeles. Friends would recommend she move back home to Boston with the baby if she came looking for help.

However, there was no turning back to her old life.

So, she started her own business.

The first con was an easy one. She had gotten a job at a diner on Wilshire in Santa Monica. An old neighbor lady, Margaret, sat for her three days a week while she got her shifts in. One guy came in one night and she gave him the eye and a smile. She got him coffee and a generous slice of pie for dessert. When the time was right, she brought him the check with her phone number scribbled on top with an arrow pointing to the back. He flipped it over and saw her lipstick imprint. His eyes shot across the room at her, and she gave him a wink, took off her apron and went out the back door.

He called her on Tuesday and asked if he could take her out. She obliged and instead of going to work, went out with him that night. She pulled in about $10,000 that year off that sucker. It was child's play for her. She imagined him waiting for her at Union Station with the tickets he'd bought to introduce his new fiancée to his family. And it was from that point that she would target the men who looked like they had money in their pockets. One scheme led to another.

Then, the phone sales calls started. It was a new marketing strategy by carpet companies. The light bulb went off in her head. This would be her new con. And the rest is history.

She heard the BMW pull up in front of her complex and gathered her belongings. Her neighbor, Mr. Wasserman, passed her in the hallway with his grocery cart and bags from Von's. She smiled at him, and he tipped his hat. He was the retired LAPD officer, and his presence made her feel safe, despite the illegal activity she ran out of her place. She'd had him over for dinner once or twice, but there was no romantic connection...it was just company. In some strange way, she felt her connection with him helped keep her cover. Who would suspect a criminal to be living across the hall from a retired cop?

Liam stood on the sidewalk with the door open and held her hand as she stepped into the front seat. He planted a gentle kiss on her cheek.

"Hey, Ma," he said, "How are you?"

"Just fine," said Mary.

"I just saw that cop go in the building."

"What cop?" asked Mary in a startled voice.

"The cop? The old guy who lives across the hall from you?"

"Oh, Mr. Wasserman," she said in a relieved tone. "Such a nice man. He's retired."

"He was a detective, you know. Worked that Valley Stalker case," added Liam.

"Huh. How do you know that?"

"I stopped at the coffee shop around the corner one time, and he told me all about it."

Liam's words bothered her for some reason. Was he spying on her? Was he asking Mr. Wasserman if she was forgetting things more often these days? She shook off the questions running around her head.

They drove down Ventura Boulevard, then he took a right on Laurel Canyon, and they made their way over the top on down to Beverly Hills.

"Where are we dining today?" asked Mary, trying to forget her newfound fear.

"I'm going to take you someplace real special, Mom," he replied.

She loved the ride up through Laurel Canyon—it was pastoral. Seven miles and just about twenty-five minutes of peace as she descended into the ritzy mansion-strewn streets, then over onto Wilshire. Liam pulled into a parking garage and shut the engine of the BMW off.

"Ma. You know I love you."

Mary smiled and was surprised with her son's sentimentality.

"Of course, sweetheart."

"Mom, I know everything," Liam said.

He did not look at her, instead staring straight ahead in the darkness of the garage

"What....do you know?" asked Mary.

"I know right now that the LAPD are in the process of issuing warrants for your arrest."

Mary felt her heart do a somersault.

"What?"

"They know everything, Ma. I've got friends who are with the police."

She looked over at Liam, stunned.

"What do they know? Everything what?"

"They've been tapping your phone, Ma. The FBI is involved. What you're doing is a federal crime. Check fraud, counterfeiting, so much more. They traced one of the donations to your bank account, Ma."

Mary laughed and shook her head. She rested her head on the comfortable leather headrest and closed her eyes. She used to be so careful, but her mind wandered these days. She had made a mistake, maybe a few lately. Her instinct was to run, back to her apartment and get the cash from underneath the floorboards, then get a cab to LAX and fly to Mexico or something—maybe Cabo San Lucas. *Escape.* She reached for the door handle and heard the click of the locks. She looked angrily back at Liam.

"I demand you open this door now!" she said with rage in her voice.

"Ma, you raised me, and you gave me a good life. I knew what you were doing since I was about five years old," he admitted. "The late nights, the cash you brought home and hid underneath the floor. My buddy from the LAPD called me yesterday. I was relieved to learn that it was just a bunch of cons."

"Now you listen to me, young man, I will not be preached to. I gave you a life. Look at you with your fancy BMW and law degree. I paid for all of it," she screamed.

Liam nodded.

"I know, and I love you for taking care of me. But you broke the law, and although I appreciate the sacrifices you made for me, they are going to throw you in prison if I don't do this right. Now, my friend, Carl Logan, is a criminal attorney and his office is right upstairs. He can probably keep your sentence down. You are a nice lady and maybe the judge will have mercy on you. But you'll need to cooperate."

Mary felt herself inside. Cooperate? Like the world had cooperated with her her whole life. What an ungrateful son she had.

Liam took her hand and she pulled it away, but he was insistent and grabbed it back.

"It's over now—all the cons, all the deception. Let me help you now. It's my turn. We are all we've got," he said.

***

She sat alone in the waiting room of an attorney's office. In her forgetful mind, she tried to piece together the series of events that led her here. She had been deceived—that was it. It was her only son who brought her to this prison room, and now, he was in the next room deciding her fate. He was just like his father—an evil man. What was his name? Charles? Chester? No, it was just Chet. She had left her one-bedroom apartment in The Valley thinking that she was going for a nice lunch with her son and now her life was upside down.

Such deception!

The voices were speaking, louder now, deep and monotone, vibrating against the other side of the wall. There was a mention of her going away someplace. Another voice popped into her head. It was her father's. "Run, Mary. Run!" he said. She looked desperately at the door and considered her escape, as if she was a trapped animal.

She would not die like her father did.

Mary thought about Mexico—Cabo San Lucas, and if it was even possible. She had been there once. The ocean water off Baja California was green and hopeful. She had worn a bikini to the pool, displaying her supple and toned body, in hopes of luring in her next victim like a black widow. That had been a good week: sunshine, margaritas—she had left there with over $10,000 in cash and goods from the hotel safe, and the Mexican police hot on her tail. That was the winter of 1968. Margaret had watched the baby while she was gone.

However, she recalled her life was not always that way.

When Mary arrived in Los Angeles in 1959, she had exactly five dollars in her purse, and little idea how she was going to survive.

Back in Boston, when she was working as a waitress in a pub in Faneuil Hall, a strange, well-dressed man told her that she had a face "made for the movies." He introduced himself as a talent scout, who was there "looking for the next big Hollywood starlet." He asked her if she had ever been on the stage, and she told him she had.

"Yes, I was in the drama club in high school," she lied.

It was a stupid fib, uncharacteristic of her at the time, but she found herself making up things more and more to deal with her current reality. The truth was, she had the records at home and sang to them all the time, alone in her room. Her father had opened a successful North End locksmith shop, but he drank the profits up and ran the business into the ground; her mother was a promiscuous and immoral woman, who slept around the neighborhood, and gave little care to her young brother and sister, whom she was forced to raise. Mary wanted to be someone else, someone more exciting, away from the poverty she grew up in with an Irish family, living in a cold-water flat in Dorchester. The man gave her his business card with an address and phone number and said to call him if she ever came to Hollywood.

In January of 1959, her father mysteriously disappeared. There were whispers in the neighborhood that her parents had secretly divorced, but when Mary confronted her mother, she'd hear nothing of it. That same winter, the Boston Savings and Loan was robbed, and the rumor was that her father was in on it—that he cracked the safe in the vault. The news came that next spring that her father had died—in a prison hospital in Philadelphia. Her mother, paralyzed with shock, had forced her to take the train down to sign for his body. She met with the coroner, who handed her the death certificate and her father's wedding ring.

"How did he die?"

"Acute alcoholic hepatitis, and tuberculosis, unfortunately," the doctor responded. "I'm assuming he was a heavy drinker."

"Yes," Mary had responded sadly. "He was."

When she returned to Boston shortly afterwards, she found that Hollywood agent's card in her dresser drawer. One day, when she was walking home from the pub, a man in a trench coat with a hat pulled down over his gray-green eyes approached her and pushed her into an alley. He reached in his coat and handed her an envelope.

"Your father wanted you to have this. He said to take care of yourself and get out of here. Leave the rest of the money for your family," he said firmly.

Then, the man disappeared around the corner.

She took the envelope home in her purse and later, when she opened it, she found a thousand dollars. After she took enough for the plane ticket to Los Angeles (about $200) she gave the rest to her mother for her and her brothers. She felt guilty even taking that much, but it was her only way out.

***

Liam emerged from the office with Logan, and they stared at the empty chair. He sprinted to the door and opened it. The hallway was empty too.

"She's gone," he shouted to Logan. "I thought you locked the damn door!"

***

The bus ride back to Studio City took a little longer than usual with the afternoon traffic. She had an extra bonnet and sunglasses in her purse—always prepared for situations like this. When she got off at Ventura Boulevard, she went directly to the payphone and called Sackostein, the printer.

"Code Red," she said into the phone and hung up.

Ten minutes later, he met her in the back alley with the Manila envelope. She opened it—the new passport was ready, along with the cash she had given him to hold. She kissed him on the cheek and handed him the note kept tucked in her wallet, written long ago, with instructions on where to find the rest of her stash. The blackmailing grifter had taught her to hide things in other places.

He promised to wire the money—and she trusted him because he truly loved her—and, like she'd said, she knew all his illegal activity that could put him away for years.

It was always smart to have leverage when you ran cons.

It was even smarter to have a plan for escape.

Love My Way

Áine set the final knife on the table; she was preparing for Conall's arrival home.

He'd be back soon, and she had planned for this surprise all day long. And to be clear, Áine was fully aware he hated surprises—everything needed to be transparent for him—but sometimes a wife must ignore a husband's predictability, habits, and idiosyncrasies, and act on her own instinct. Conall wrote scripts and directed the behaviors of his characters; she often felt like she was one of them that he could control the fate of. It bothered her greatly. Last year, she had tried a surprise birthday party for him, but something horrible happened when they had gotten home—he had slapped her hard in the face, so hard that it had broken her nose. He'd been so apologetic and loving after, and it never happened again. However, this surprise was quite different.

Áine moved back into the kitchen, glancing out the window and studying the pastoral backyard. Pink and white magnolia flowers bloomed from the trees behind the home. She'd felt restless and rather feral lately. Perhaps it was her body adapting to the time change: everything seemed different in the West. She told herself that it began the day the coyote had killed their beloved dog. It wandered into their backyard, from somewhere out in the canyon, and found their puppy, snapping it up in its jaws. Áine had sprinted from the back deck, charging it with a frying pan and striking it before it sprinted away into the woods. When she looked back down, there was blood on the black pan. Sobbing, she walked back to the house.

"We'll get another one, my little songbird," Conall had said. "Everything is replaceable."

She knew this statement was false, and truly despised Conall's little pet names for her. He treated her like a little girl sometimes. Time had passed, and she'd gotten over it but there was no new dog yet. It made her sad to think about it all. All her innocence had faded the day of her puppy's death, as if it had been swallowed up in an earthquake that shook the very foundation of their canyon home.

Still, she loved her husband, and Áine knew all her moves tonight. She'd intentionally bought a leg of mutton for dinner—it was his favorite, after all. It was a little bit of Ireland away from home. He'd been working so hard lately and had been since they relocated to Santa Monica from Dublin. They lived a white-laced life, in a safe neighborhood north of Montana Avenue, off San Vicente Boulevard. However, there had been some break-ins lately, and Conall had lectured her to keep the doors locked when he was gone.

"I don't want some drug addict burglar breaking into our home, striking you over the head with a bat or something, just to steal some diamonds," he had remarked a few days before.

Their neighbor, the wife of a famous screenwriter, had encountered an intruder, a homeless man with a knife, who climbed in her bedroom window. She fought him off with her husband's 9-iron. Áine reminded herself of the security company appointment the next morning—the previous owner had disconnected the cameras due to the expense of the yearly commitment; her weekly yoga would have to be rescheduled. She was grateful that Conall had always worried about her well-being. He joked that she was "his little doll from Dublin in her California dream dollhouse." Those words bothered her even more than his pet names, but in many ways, he was correct. She'd gone from her father's home to his, no better than Nora from Ibsen's *A Doll's House*. She took the leg of mutton out of the refrigerator and set it on the cutting board, next to the cleaver. The defrosting meat hit the board with tremendous thud; it startled her with its leverage. She began her preparations for the evening by seasoning the leg of mutton with herbs and spices. Áine wanted to show what Conall meant to her on this evening.

Her father had been a butcher back in the day, so she knew how to handle sharp objects. Áine found the shiny green bottle of Jameson in the liquor cabinet and set it on the table, pouring half a glass for Conall. She then located a tall can of Guinness and set it next to it. These were for him; there would be no intoxication for her tonight. Her news would suffice as delirium. For tonight was a night of celebration, and it would be all about them. She touched her belly, and the loneliness that she had felt moving so far away from Ireland would be over. Fervor overcame her and she laughed. She hoped he was prepared for the news she had always handled them in stride her whole life. Nothing shocked her, she always managed to hold her composure, always brave under pressure. She had been good with the field hockey stick—the leading scorer at St. Brigid's Convent School; the nuns had taught her a thing or two about boxing her own corner. Her swing had tremendous clout, and her father warned her about the injury she could cause someone. However, her days of athletics and field hockey were over now; she focused on spin classes and personal training, instead, but she would have to take a break from that in a few months. Her muscles were strong, but she maintained a lean, sinewy figure. She imagined herself pushing the pram up and down Montana Ave. soon. It was stylish in Santa Monica to have a baby. You'd think that there was a slew of single moms with the pram traffic there, and no sign of the high-earning, successful Hollywood husbands accompanying them.

Conall was directing movies now, and *The Hollywood Reporter* had declared that if he had another hit, he would become "King Conall of Tinseltown." She kept the home and did what rich wives did in L.A. There was tennis at the Riviera Country Club, and lunch with the girls over at the Jonathon Club. Conall made sure they belonged to all the right clubs and rubbed elbows with all the right people in the business. It was overwhelming at times. She thought of what her friends from school were doing back in Ireland, their mundane lives, filled with cloudy skies and rain. It was depressing there. Her dreams started coming true when she had left her village in Wexford for college in Dublin. It was there that she had met this handsome, aspiring young screenwriter and filmmaker named Conall O'Neill. His pure Irish complexion—pale skin and dark hair—attracted her. He looked like a taller Colin Farrell, but it was more than that. It was his dark sense of humor and charisma that won her over.

She heard Conall's Audi A8 pull into the circular driveway and went to the mirror to apply the final touches to her face. She was twenty-nine years old, but she looked younger and desirable. At a drunken Fourth of July party at the Beach Club, one of Conall's screenwriter friends had tried to kiss her once, but her fidelity was strong and pushed him away. Conall seemed to have little concern when she related the story saying only, "These Americans are different than you, especially the ones in Hollywood." She only had eyes for her husband, and she was certain of his desire for her.

As she walked toward the door to greet him, she felt anxiety in her stomach. There was one actress whom Conall seemed overly attached to. She was blond and had plastic breast implants and a shapely, hourglass figure. Áine despised when the spoke of her; perhaps it was jealousy. She shook off the twinge in her stomach.

When Áine opened the door, Conall was still talking on his phone. He gave her the one-second finger, continuing his conversation as if she were invisible. She waited patiently and went back to the kitchen to prepare the defrosting mutton. She turned the oven on to four-hundred degrees and realized she had inanely forgotten the vegetables and potatoes. Looking at the time, she calculated it would take half an hour roundtrip to drive down to Whole Foods for the sides. How stupid of her! She hadn't planned on this. Conall came in the house and stared at the table.

"What's all this?" he said, sounding a bit irritated.

She turned and smiled.

"Sit down and have a drink, darling," Áine said.

"I'm not staying," he said.

She should have known what was coming. He'd be off to some "forgotten" Hollywood event that he neglected to tell her about.

"I'm preparing dinner and I have some news," she said, beaming.

Conall looked at her blankly. His phone buzzed and he looked at it.

"I'm sorry, darling. I have to take this."

He walked in the other room and fell into a discussion. When he came back in the kitchen, she turned and smiled.

"Everything okay?" she asked.

"Sit down," Conall said with an irritated tone.

"Why? What's wrong?"

"Darling, just sit," he insisted.

He pulled out a chair and pointed at the seat firmly.

The next few moments were full of frenzy and disorientation for Áine. She felt like she was floating above the room, watching a strange husband and wife in conversation. Conall spoke quite eloquently, as if he was pitching a new project filled with wonderful promise, presenting the benefits for both.

It took about five minutes, although it felt like longer, and when he was finished, he finally picked up the glass of Jameson and drank it all down. He set the emptied glass down on the table with a force that startled her as much as the frozen mutton had earlier.

"Of course, you can stay here. The home is yours. I'll make sure that you are cared for. Money is no object," he promised. "You know I'll always love you, but the heart wants what the heart wants. Life is short. We all have to live."

She nodded and stared at his empty glass. Then, as if it was instinct, she took it and poured her own glass of the Jameson, drinking it down.

"Sweetheart, please say something," he begged her.

Áine said nothing. It was not a time for words.

Finally, she rose and went into the dining room to stare out at the backyard, looking out at the spot where her puppy had been snatched by the coyote. Conall's phone buzzed again, and he was back on another call.

It was probably that actress, she thought.

Escape.

This was the word that whirled in her brain right now. What would she do? There was a baby coming. Her mind was racing. Panic and rage raced through her veins. She walked into the kitchen, as if commanded by a foreign and most unnatural voice and picked up the frozen mutton on the way to the living room.

Conall was facing the window and was laughing on the phone like a giddy schoolgirl. Áine raised her arms high in the air, then swung the hard, frozen leg of mutton with tremendous leverage toward his skull. The sound was like an aluminum bat striking a frozen snowman.

He turned and looked at her, confused, as blood poured down his face. He dropped his phone and it slammed against the hardwood floor.

"But...why?" whispered Conall

Then, his lifeless body slammed to the floor. Áine dropped the mutton to the floor beside his, then reached down and picked up his phone and listened.

"Darling? Are you there? I've lost you. What was that sound?" said the actress's voice.

Áine hung up the phone and dropped it back on the ground. Picking up her frozen weapon, she returned to the kitchen, and stuck the leg of mutton back on the tray, then stuffed it in the oven. She located the keys to her Land Rover. Remembering that she had sides to pick up: vegetables and potatoes.

As she drove down 24th to Montana, she saw a mother walking with a pram and smiled. She turned into the parking lot of Whole Foods and found a space. She made sure she was visible on all the cameras; there was no dreadful fear or nervousness—only a sense of liberation and redemption. Inside she had several conversations with the staff: they all knew her. When she had her potatoes, bag of fresh salad, and carrots, she stood in line and even greeted a few of her tennis friends in line.

Back at home, as expected, she saw a Santa Monica police car sitting in her driveway. The response was quicker than she'd estimated. She pulled the Land Rover in and got out with the grocery bags.

"Hello? May I help you?" Áine asked

"Ma'am, do you live here?' said the officer.

"Why, yes. What seems to be the issue?" she asked.

"We received a wellness-call from a concerned party. Is this Conall O'Neill's home as well?"

"Yes, he's, my husband. He should still be inside. That's his car. I just ran to the store," she said.

"About how long ago?"

"Half an hour.

"Was he home yet?"

"No. Why? What's happened?" she asked in a concerned tone "I forgot the sides and ran out to Whole Foods."

The officer nodded.

"Mind if I take a look inside?" he asked.

"No, of course," Áine said.

They proceeded through the front door. The officer stayed in front of her and unbuckled his holster.

"Are you cooking something?"

"Yes. A celebratory dinner. I put some mutton in before I left," she said. "It's in the oven now."

He nodded and proceeded into the living room. Then he saw Conall's body.

"Stay back, ma'am," he shouted. "You don't want to see this."

She backed out the door into the driveway and sat on the steps. Within a minute, two more police cars arrived on the scene, and officers ran past her into the house.

They'd figure it out, and she'd have this baby in prison. Conall was so selfish, having an affair with that actress. She knew he couldn't resist the temptations of Hollywood.

Finally, an officer came out. He was in plain clothes and smiled at her.

"Ma'am, I'm Detective Wasserman. Could you tell me your name?

"Áine O'Neill," she heard herself say. "I'm his wife."

"Ma'am, we believe your husband was murdered. How long has it been since you last saw him?" he asked.

"Um...this morning. When he left for work. I must have just missed him when I ran out," she said.

He nodded.

"Could you show me some ID?" he asked.

"Yes, but I've left my purse in the kitchen."

She got up and followed the detective into the kitchen.

"Oh," she said, laughing nervously. "No, it's in the car."

She started that way, but he held his hands up.

"Let me get it," he said. "Stay right here."

His tone seemed firm and untrusting. He walked briskly back toward the front door. She turned to see the two glasses on the table and quickly grabbed her's, washed it out, and stuck it in the cabinet. She studied the table. There was the Jameson, the unopened Guinness, and the table settings left. Those would be easily explained. She went to the oven and saw that there was fifteen minutes left on the timer.

The leg of mutton would be cooked soon.

The detective came back and handed her the purse.

"I won't lie to you, but that smells delicious. What was...is.... the occasion," he inquired.

She found her wallet and handed him the ID, smiling sadly.

"We were celebrating. I'm expecting," Áine said.

"Oh, congratulations," Wasserman began, but stopped when he realized the full impact of her words.

He studied her ID, then handed back the wallet, and she returned it to her purse.

"So, how long have you two been married?" he inquired.

"Five years," she said, reminding herself to choke up a bit.

She used the revelation of the affair to create the sadness.

"Wow. And do you know anybody who would want to harm your husband?" he asked.

She thought.

"Well, there was this actress who was unhappy with the fact that he was married, you might know her."

She said her name.

"Oh yes, she's very famous. I saw her last two films," he remarked.

"Do you think they were...."

"Having an affair?" she blurted. "Not that I'm aware. Conall was always very loyal to me. We met in college. We've been together for ten years total."

The buzzer went off from behind her.

"It's ready. The mutton is cooked," she said. "Would you like some, Detective? It will just be thrown out if you don't eat it."

Two police officers came in and observed Áine setting the juicy dinner on the platter. She reached in the cupboard and took out some more plates and set the silverware down.

"Please, eat, Officers," Áine pleaded, forcing tears to run down her face.

This was her greatest performance as a wife. She felt the delirium returning to her.

"We are all going to be here for a while, right? I have nowhere to be. Conall would have loved a meal like this. It was his favorite. You would be doing me a personal favor if you ate this."

The detective rubbed his chin, as if he had never contemplated doing such a thing at the scene of a homicide. After a moment, he nodded to the officers to sit down and eat. They happily complied and dug into the meal.

Áine watched from behind the men, crying tears of joy as they ate.

Suddenly, she recalled Conall's words when her dog died.

"Everything is replaceable," she whispered.

Evaluation Day

On this Monday morning, Gabriel was hyper-focused on one thing: his first period observation with Principal Edward DePinko.

Everything seemed to be in perfect harmony. His coffee was steaming hot, the sun was shining in the perfect blue sky, and even the traffic from suburban Massachusetts into Rhode Island was surprisingly light and moving steadily. That's primarily why the bullet that came searing through his back window absolutely infuriated him and ruined his morning. I mean, he hated being late for school—especially on an evaluation day.

"Sniper," he shouted, as he simultaneously calculated the velocity and make of the bullet. .50 BMG. Travels at 2065 miles per hour covering 3029 feet per second. His brain seemed to see the bullet in slow motion as it ricocheted off the hood of the silver Audi, leaving a nasty scrape.

Immediately, he felt that old rage rising inside him, one that was quite primal. He thought of the cost of the body-shop repairs for the damages.

Gabriel had taken the English position at Kennedy High School upon his return from an "extended" stay in Europe, and he just wanted to settle into this new career like any new teacher and be normal. His handler felt teaching was the best option—too many people were looking for him—he needed to blend in and become a chameleon in blue blazer, tie, and tan slacks. No one would believe a world-renowned assassin would be working at a high school. He took summer institutes in AP Language and Literature to sharpen his fake resume. However, to maintain his cover, it required winning the respect, approval, and recommendation of his evaluator–Principal DePinko–if he wanted to make this cover seem real. His handler was adamant that tenure needed to be achieved to ensure he kept his identity safe, to blend back into society. However, as he neared the busy 95/195 interchange in Providence, a second bullet pierced the back window of his Audi, spraying glass this time on the dark leather seats, as it proceeded past his right ear, then out the center of the front windshield.

However, the rage was far deeper than a sniper attack, or the consideration of the price gouging at an Audi dealership, and he knew it. This rage had begun the day his father died quite suddenly when he was eleven years old. He had not felt a rage that reminded him of this loss for almost three years, when he eliminated the target in London from the rooftop of a hotel. After the second bullet, he swerved around in traffic, his mind replayed the image of him aiming his rifle on a rooftop in Berlin, Germany, as he pulled the trigger to eliminate a despicable target who had done unspeakable things in the trafficking of children around the world. Yes—he knew what it felt like on the other side of the situation. Gabriel collected himself from the initial shock, then negotiated the exit, never an easy task in busy southbound 95 traffic. Then, as if he was in a parking lot practicing three point turns, he effortlessly swung the car around toward where the bullet had come from.

Normally, he would have been well past Providence River Bridge, over the border, and have made it into Massachusetts, toward Fall River, but now he would be running late today—that could cost him ten minutes. And add to it all, this bullet was making him even more late than he usually was. The Audi sped directly back into oncoming traffic as horns blared, and cars swerved. He spotted the black Suburban with the sniper still hanging out the window, preparing for his third shot. The assassins always seemed to pick the oversized, black SUVs with tinted windows. So predictable, he thought.

Gabriel now saw the shooter was hoping to get one final kill shot in—probably trained in some Mickey Mouse camp run by some Communists in a third-world country. Sniper training these days was at the same level as ordinary people with smart phones calling themselves photographers. Amateur hour.

He knew their moves. In his mind, he knew the sniper predicted he'd attempt to finish him off and would try to escape to T.F. Greene Airport in Warwick and be on a commercial international flight, probably to Ireland, before they dredged his Audi out of the Providence River. The images of this scenario enraged him even further, and he swung the car to the right and followed in hot pursuit. He leaned forward and popped the glove box and found his old Glock 22 handgun wedged underneath the registration and the car manual. He had kept it locked and loaded there in the box just in case someone came looking for him.

The fact he knew for certain was that no one wanted Gabriel to catch them. These pricks were assassins for hire, and he had to dispose of them—quickly—because he knew there would be more coming for him. And he would not be even later to school dealing with their incompetence. The Audi caught up to the Suburban quickly, and the driver turned in astonishment. There was a look of fear and failure on his face, and he commanded his driver to slam the SUV into the Audi, which only infuriated Gabriel further, if that was even possible.

"You are dead," Gabriel said as he mouthed the words to them. "You hear me?"

He powered his window down with his left hand and fired with his right, unloading the Glock, hitting both the driver and passenger with two head shots. The car coasted for a moment, then started swerving to the left. Gabriel watched with satisfaction as the Suburban slammed into the wall, then flipped over the bridge, end over end into the depths of the Providence River.

He set the Glock down on the passenger seat and took a deep breath.

This wasn't the first time they had tried to eliminate him. He'd come out of the shower in his hotel room in Moscow and happened to catch an assassin in his room donning a knife. If it wasn't for his glance in a wall mirror, he'd have been a goner that time. Another time in London, he'd met a beautiful woman and gone back to her place, only to realize that she had been hired to kill him. That was a tough one, but he had found her B&T Station Six-45 8 RD 45 ACP pistol with a suppressor in the medicine cabinet, he'd had no choice. Initially he didn't suspect a thing. After all, Gabriel was a good-looking guy, but later he found it so odd that that girl had come up to him in the pub, out of the blue.

Around Fall River, he collected himself and saw that it was 7:10 AM. He'd just make it to class on time, so he went over the Rhetorical Analysis lesson in his head. He was going with Margaret Thatcher's eulogy for Ronald Reagan. It portrayed Reagan as the hero who won the Cold War, as well as a close friend and confidant of Thatcher. It was always an engaging piece to break down. At least in his mind.

He looked back down at the Glock on the passenger seat and considered the witnesses. He'd have to call the Colonel to clean up the mess—hell, he probably already knew. Usually, if something was going down, the Colonel would call him the night before. This was a stealth hit. Although, the Colonel resided in a nursing home on the East Side of Providence, his connections to the Rhode Island State Police and FBI ran deep. The Colonel would be able to spin a situation in the right direction within an hour before his game of shuffleboard.

The burner phone was in the glove box, as well, and Gabriel made the call and gave the Colonel the details as he weaved through the school parking lot. The Colonel was on his way, and Gabriel had an evaluation to nail.

***

Principal Edward Salvatore DePinko grew up in East Boston around Italian mobsters but was not one himself. When he was a kid, his father got sick and went to the hospital, and he and his mom were "taken care of." One of his earliest memories was being sent downstairs to pay the rent, and the bookies carrying him around declaring, "The kid wants to place a bet!" He realized he was smart early on and did well in school, went to college, and became a teacher and hockey coach at the high school level. Someone put it in his head that he could be an administrator and a guy in the North End was able to produce a fake master's degree and $100 later, he was licensed at age twenty-three. By the time Gabriel showed up, DePinko had been in the education industry for thirty years. He was bitter and irritable and didn't like young teachers. Gabriel was twenty-five years old and was happy with his career change. DePinko hired him, but in some dark, fatherly sort of way, he wanted to mold him into the educator he thought he should be.

Gabriel looked up and saw DePinko slip into the back of his classroom with his laptop, almost like a serpent slithering into position before it tried to envelop its prey. He made his way through the lesson, breaking down Margaret Thatcher's eulogy for Ronald Reagan in manageable parts. The students seemed to comprehend it fine, but he knew he'd have to check with them for understanding—DePinko's pet peeve if you forgot to mention that to the students. There had to be discernable evidence that the students were comprehending, especially in an AP class. Scores were always part of the evaluation.

Halfway through the lesson, the rage returned to his body. DePinko pulled out the green book: the book of state standards.

His histrionic squint, from his dark, brownish oily brown skin, and animated flipping of the pages of the green book sent an intense fervor, a tick or two below the attempted assassination by the Russians this morning, through Gabriel's body. It was as if he had to show the evidence of good teaching before his long speech down in his office following the observation.

The bell finally rang.

DePinko sat and continued typing as Gabriel collected the half-sheets of exit tickets on the desks. Finally, he looked up.

"Oh—is this your prep period?" he asked.

"No, I have a small ELA 10 class coming in third period," Gabriel replied. "I'm off last period."

DePinko got up and looked around the room as if he was looking for a key element to include in his report.

"Place is a mess," he said. "Felt sorry for the kids. It's in disarray, those papers," he remarked. "Gotta clean this mess up. No place for kids to learn."

Gabriel imagined himself with the Glock 22 in his hands, firing at the Suburban only a few hours ago. He had two perfect headshots—the passenger first, then the driver. He wondered if someone had run over the rifle that dropped out the window as it bounced against the asphalt, maybe even some truck on its way to New Bedford. However, as he aimed his gun in this daydream, it was DePinko leaning out the window with the rifle firing back at him.

"Goodman, you with me? Asked why you were late today."

He snapped his fingers in front of Gabriel's face. Gabriel set the papers down on the desk.

"Sorry—yeah, my commute through Providence can get a little... complicated," he said.

"Traffic?"

"Something like that. Lots of road rage out there."

"Got to be careful. Maybe leave a little bit earlier. That's what I do. Ten minutes makes all the difference. Otherwise, I have to drive like a mad man to get here. People are distracted...they'll kill you,"

DePinko said. "I don't like that feeling. It's unprofessional to be late. Keep that in mind."

"Thanks," Gabriel replied. "I will."

"You don't want to have a target on your back," DePinko said.

Gabriel looked at him strangely. What an unusual choice of words.

"Target...on my back?"

DePinko smirked.

"Not literally. Figuratively. You're an English teacher. You get symbolism and what not," he said. "You keep showing up late and are unorganized, you become a target...you understand?"

"I'll keep that in mind," Gabriel said.

DePinko looked around once more and shook his head.

"Come down to my office at 2:40 PM. and we'll go over your evaluation."

He turned and walked out. Gabriel sighed as DePinko disappeared into the hallway. He felt a buzzing in his pocket and pulled out the burner phone. It was the Colonel.

"How are we looking, Colonel?"

"We took care of it. How are you, more importantly?"

"Little shaken up."

"Look out the window of your classroom. The one facing the parking lot."

Gabriel went to his classroom window. He had parked underneath a tree, so the bullet holes were not visible to the naked eye. A white SafeShield truck was parked next to it, and a man was there working on the windshield replacement.

"Nice. Thanks, Colonel."

"How'd that big observation go?" he asked.

"It is what it is," Gabriel responded. "This guy is a real asshole."

"Well, don't kill him. Do a good job. This is the perfect cover," he said.

"If it's so good, how did these guys find me?"

"Fluke. We're not even sure who they are yet. We are going to have to move your residence. Less to do with the job, more to do with your living situation," he said. "Our intel says these guys flew into Boston this morning. My Providence PD connection is getting back to me once they fish them out of the Providence River. You just go about your business. We may have to get you a new car," he said.

"Too bad. I like that Audi," Gabriel responded.

"It's a real douche-mobile. I hate Audi drivers. Don't know why you picked it," replied the Colonel. "You're not James Bond: you're supposed to be a high school teacher. We'll get you a Chevy. Besides, you'll go broke with the damn maintenance costs on those German makes. You ever think of Cadillac or a Grand Marquis? Very classy, yet reliable, vehicles."

"I'm not a loan shark or a poker player. Jesus, Colonel."

Behind him there was a knock on his door. It was Casey Cipriano, his closest teacher friend.

"Colonel, I gotta go," he said, hanging up quickly.

Casey Cipriano walked in. She was in her twenties and pretty. Gabriel had just turned twenty-five the previous summer—he recalled celebrating in Paris with a glass of champagne at the top of the Eiffel Tower—before he pushed two Saudis, who were funding ISIS, over the rails. If circumstances were different, he'd ask her on a date, take her to the top of the Eiffel Tower. Obviously not push her over. A different celebration altogether. It had been hard to begin relationships considering his profession.

"Wow, Gabriel, I'm surprised to see you," she said.

"Yeah, I ran into some killer traffic on the way in," he remarked.

"Nothing too serious, I hope."

"Ah...just a couple of guys in a SUV who tried to kill me," he said. "You just want to shoot those types of drivers, you know?"

"Shoot them?"

Casey paused and looked at him, then they simultaneously started laughing.

"How'd the evaluation with DePinko go?" she asked.

"Feel like I got shot in the back," Gabriel said. "He said the room was a mess."

She laughed and looked around.

"It kind of is," she said, studying the stacks of papers. "You realize we have to correct these essays and hand them back.

"Yeah, rough morning. I'll work on it this period. Got to debrief with the boss last block," he said.

"Well good luck, Gabriel," she said. "I'm pulling for you."

He paused for a moment and thought about just asking her out, maybe for dinner up on Federal Hill this weekend. But he hesitated as she turned and walked out the door.

He didn't want to invite her into his dangerous world.

***

Gabriel was driving back home. The windshield was fixed, but he could see the gouge on the hood that the sniper's bullet left. DePinko had given him Unsatisfactory. Again. He wanted him out—he obviously felt threatened by Gabriel for some reason. There seemed that there was no way to get this guy to like him. He swung his car to the right and exited to the East Side of Providence to the Broken Branches Assisted Living Center off of Hope Street. It was an upscale rest home where people could come and go: retired Brown professors, wealthy Rhode Islanders, and one of the greatest cleaners the spy world had every known: the Colonel.

Patrick Furlong Bradley was the Colonel's real name. He'd started out as a Rhode Island State Trooper, but with his takedown of the La Cuesta Nostra—the mafia—especially the Bordino Crime Family based in Cranston, Rhode Island, he had established his brazen reputation. They tried to kill him, his family, even his elderly parents in their rest home with a bomb. However, they failed, and The Colonel had put them all behind bars. The FBI and CIA heavily recruited him because of the similar tactics that terrorist groups were using. By the time he was forty years old, The Colonel had retired and moved away from Rhode Island to jolly old London. His parents had passed of natural causes, and he was collaborating with MI5 and Interpol by disposing of the evils of terrorism across the globe. However, it was Providence that pulled him back home, and it was there that he took on a very different role, one that led to the recruitment of a young law enforcement officer named Gabriel Michael Goodman.

It was bingo night, and Gabriel walked through the lobby with a six-pack of Guinness and found The Colonel next to his bingo date. He looked up and smiled.

"Oh, Gabriel," he said. "Meet Margaret"

He shook hands with an old lady who smiled at him.

"He's a tall one," she remarked as she set the winning chip on O. "Bingo!'

The crowd groaned as The Colonel planted a kiss on her cheek.

"You'll have to excuse us, Peg," he said. "I've got to talk to my nephew for a bit."

The Colonel got up with his walker, and Gabriel retrieved the Guinness as they walked back to his room. There he put the other four tall cans in the fridge and cracked open two and set one in front of The Colonel's TV tray by his recliner.

"Turn on the TV and put the volume up a bit," The Colonel said as he collapsed in the recliner.

He sipped the Guinness and held up a toast.

"Slainte! To your long life."

Gabriel sat down and sipped his Guinness as well.

"Shouldn't you be lesson planning?" asked The Colonel.

"Whatever. I got an Unsatisfactory from that loser. What's the update?" Gabriel asked. "Who were those fuckers?"

"Turns out that they tracked you," The Colonel said. "From your visits here and because of someone you work with."

He stood up and lifted a cushion in the recliner to reveal a large envelope. The Colonel handed it to Gabriel.

"DePinko?" asked Gabriel.

"No."

Gabriel stared at the photograph in front of him. It was Casey Cipriano.

"What's this?"

"She figured out your cover. She's the granddaughter of Gelindo 'Sonny Boy' Bordino. The Don I put away for life thirty years ago."

Gabriel felt that rage rise again: this time it was the rage of betrayal.

"She's the head of the family now. She runs things. Those two guys in the SUV? They were from Sicily, not Russia. They were hired to take you and me out. She thinks you are my nephew."

Gabriel slid the picture back in the envelope. He felt the dagger deep in his back...or was it in his heart?

"Oh, one other thing," began The Colonel. "Turns out your DePinko is a real slime ball."

"How so?" asked Gabriel.

"He's been using these city kids to sell drugs. Basically, he preys on the kids without fathers and gets them to push pills on the street," he said.

"You've got to be kidding me."

"Second set of photos and phone records are right there. I know you hate the guy for other reasons, but he is a detriment to society," said The Colonel. "I can bust him with my connections if you'd like."

Gabriel looked at the evidence in front him. He was wired to foresee this in people—it was in his DNA—an ancient gift from his

Irish ancestors trying to fight the sacking Romans or Vikings. This was his fate—to punish those who were inhumane. He thought of himself as the hand of God.

"You know what you have to do," said the Colonel. "Then, unfortunately, you gotta disappear again."

Gabriel nodded as he watched The Colonel finish his can of Guinness. He got up slowly, set the chair back at the table, and walked out the door.

***

There was nothing like coming to a job, knowing that what you did today didn't matter because you were quitting.

Gabriel moved through the lesson on Caesar Chavez's speech on MLK's 10th Anniversary of his death, talking about his plea to migrant workers to resist violent protests.

"So, the overall purpose of the message from Chavez was that to gain support from the public, the migrant workers needed to protest peacefully. He cites Gandhi and MLK as leaders who did this successfully."

Jose Correia raised his hand in the front row. He was a smart kid.

"But, Mr. G, isn't violence the only way that people get the message sometimes?"

Gabriel forced a smile and thought of the Glock and silencer tucked in the back of his school pants.

"That's the point, Jose," he said. "Chavez says, 'The rich may have money, but the poor have time.'"

"That don't make no sense, Mr. G," said Jose.

"You don't have to believe Chavez," said Gabriel. "You're doing a rhetorical analysis here. You just must identify the device and write about its purpose and effect. Understand?"

The bell rang and Gabriel thought of Hemingway's *For Whom the Bell Tolls,* although he preferred his short story "The Killers" over most of his novels. Then again, the next chapter of his life was probably going to be like *The Sun Also Rises* as he might be able to catch the Festival of San Fermin in Pamplona, for the running of the bulls.

He walked down the crowded hallway. He planned to get DePinko in his office during lunch—he always hid there like a rat—probably planning his drug mule business. Society would be better without him, and Gabriel was still pissed off about those two "Unsatisfactory" evaluations.

Casey Cipriano's demise would be a little more complicated. The faculty room was not a good option: too many folks making copies. Lunch duty: kids were around. He thought about going to her apartment and doing it, but he had a 3 PM flight out of TF Green to Dublin so he didn't want to have to go all the way back to Providence. Traffic would be a nightmare.

He passed the school security guard as he made his way toward the cafeteria. Mr. Jenkins had served three tours in Afghanistan, and he always wondered if he knew more than his smile and greeting revealed. Soldiers have these gut feelings, the kind that pop up at checkpoints when the insurgents hide in plain sight with the civilians. Gabriel greeted him and reached back to feel the Glock underneath his coat.

"Mr. Goodman, how are we today? You teachin' those kids to write real good?" said Jenkins.

Gabriel laughed, then felt something very odd happen. The Glock slid down the back of his pants and down his pant leg and fell on the floor.

Jenkins' smile faded and he looked down at the gun oddly.

Gabriel knew there was no time for cordialities, so he leaned in and clocked Jenkins. To his dismay, the punch did little.

"Now stay where you are, Mr. Goodman," said Jenkins, looking at him intensely.

Gabriel weighed his options. If he fought Jenkins, the police would be here in minutes. He needed that gun to finish the job, but Jenkins suddenly kicked it, and they watched as it slid across the tile floor.

"I knew it," screamed Jenkins. "You ain't no teacher; you're a goddamn hitman! I pegged you from the beginning."

Without another thought, Gabriel dove at him and they crashed against the wall. Jenkins quickly reversed things with his military training and put him in a headlock. Gabriel struggled, like a feral animal caught in a trap, trying in vain to get out.

"You fucking cowards hiding behind your guns," screamed Jenkins. "How's hand-to-hand combat feel?"

Gabriel felt faint, he was cutting off the blood to his head. His oxygen levels were dropping. He saw the gun ten feet away and flailed toward it, but the choke hold was too much. He felt something in his right pocket as his hands brushed his leg. Ten more seconds and he would be a goner.

He grabbed the Bic ballpoint pen, flung the cap off, slamming the tip into Jenkins lower back, then up toward his neck. He felt his grip loosen, and then a scream of agony. Jenkins fell back. Blood was spurting everywhere.

Gabriel dove toward the gun, grabbed it and pointed it at Jenkins, who was grabbing the pen stuck into his throat. Blood pooled on the floor. He felt badly because it would be a big cleanup for the custodians.

He put two bullets in Jenkins's head and tucked the gun in the back of his pants as he ran down the hallway and out the back door, just as the lunch period bell rang.

***

By the time Gabriel hit Rte. 195 North, the sirens were all around him, but heading in the opposite direction. He grabbed his phone, dialed, and The Colonel finally picked up.

"Sorry, I'm at shuffleboard," he apologized. "What's up? I'm surprised to be hearing from you."

"I dropped my gun and the security guard…I had to eliminate him," he said.

"Oh Jesus," said the Colonel.

"The jobs are not finished."

"Well get back there and finish them," shouted the Colonel. "You do understand that we have a shortage of assassins due to the pandemic, right? The government makes it easier to stay home then go out and kill people. It's a real shame."

"I am not going back in that school. Cops are all over that place by now. It's over, Colonel," he shouted. "I'm done being an English teacher. I've got to get out of the country."

"Well, you weren't a very good one anyway," he shot back.

"Fuck off. I did my best. I can't help it if my main profession got in the way."

"Okay, I guess I can take care of this. You'll have to go away for a while," he said. "Disappearing is what you do best. But since you didn't finish off Cipriano, you'll always be looking over your shoulder. Stay out of Italy. Have you been to Scandinavia?"

Gabriel thought about it. He didn't want to live that way. One last kill and he could be free.

"Okay, okay, Colonel," he said. "I'll take care of her. I'm going to her house now. I will eliminate the threat when she gets home from school."

"And I will take care of your drug dealing degenerate principal," he remarked. "We have a boat cruise out of that area tomorrow. I'll swing by after. Oh, and I will re-book for tomorrow morning out of Boston. How does Copenhagen sound?"

Gabriel hung up the burner phone and tossed it out the window. He watched as an Amazon truck ran over and demolished it. The pieces flew everyplace.

***

He knew he had to ditch the car.

It took a few hours, but he sold the Audi to a guy off Smith Street in North Providence for $10,000, a steal with only 40,000 miles on it. The guy threw in a 2002 Subaru Impreza with 187,000 miles on it, so he could make his last kill, then get to the airport. He felt that he had suckered the guy since Audis all had major issues pop up as they aged. Parts and labor were outrageous.

Gabriel drove to the East Side and found Casey's apartment off Wayland Square. He shut off the lights and waited in the dark with the Glock on his lap until he heard the key unlock the door. She came in and he clicked on the lamp next to him, watching her jump.

"Jesus. Gabriel—they are looking for you," she blurted. "What did you do today?'

"Take a seat," he said, nodding to the chair across from him. "And let me see those hands."

She sat down slowly, holding her hands up by her shoulders.

"What's going on?"

"You know what's going on. You tried to kill me the other day. I know it all. I know who are. I know what you do," he said.

"I don't know what you are talking about."

He'd been through this ruse before. The target tried to control the situation, pretending like they were clueless. Making the assassin feel like they were making a mistake, that they had bad intel. Maybe someone was using them to do their dirty work.

Liars. Phonies.

"This will be quick and painless. I wish I could make it hurt a little bit more, but I have a plane to catch," he said.

"Someone is using you," Casey pleaded. "They've told you lies."

Gabriel laughed.

"So, you are not the granddaughter of Gelindo Bordino?"

"No. Who is that?"

Gabriel laughed again.

"Man, you are really good at this."

"Good at what? My grandfather's last names were Cipriano and Bradley," she said, starting to cry. "Did you kill Mr. Jenkins, Gabriel?"

Crocodile tears. She was good, he admitted to himself. Bradley, that was The Colonel's last name. He hesitated.

"What's your grandfather's full name—the Bradley side?"

"Patrick."

His brain was swimming in an ocean of confusion. Why would The Colonel want him to kill his own granddaughter?

"He must be using you, Gabriel."

Gabriel laughed. Typical desperation. He steadied his gun.

"Why would he do that? He is like a father to me."

"Because" she managed to get out. "I do what you do."

"No, you're not. You are a high school French teacher."

"No—he trained me to be an assassin too," she cried. "Remember that vacation I took to Hawaii last Christmas?"

Gabriel did. It was with a prick in his department who had been Teacher of the Year, Ivy League guy, Griffin Coogan.

"Yeah?"

"Well, I wasn't in Hawaii, I was in Singapore."

"Doing what?"

"I was flown over from Maui to kill two Chinese spies. The Colonel, himself, trained me to do this."

"Why'd you do it?"

"Because that's who I am now. Well, that, and it paid $50,000."

Gabriel nodded. Starting teacher salaries were low, and rents on the East Side of Providence were through the roof. No other choice but to supplement your income.

"So, your other grandfather is not in prison for life?" he asked.

"No, he's a deacon at our church. The Colonel moved into Broken Branches as a cover. He is the brains behind an international spy and assassin ring."

Gabriel wasn't sure.

"What happened in Singapore?"

"I didn't do the job," she cried. "They had a baby."

"Baby?"

"Yeah, they had this little infant, and when I got into their hotel room, I couldn't pull the trigger," she said.

Gabriel had been there. He had a hard time when children were involved too. It wasn't their fault that their parents were spies or assassins.

"People are dead because of my decision. Orders came down to eliminate me. He is using you because he doesn't have the guts to kill his own granddaughter," she moaned. "Can't you see?"

Gabriel did see. Orders came down. They always do in situations like these. You just couldn't trust anybody these days. But The Colonel had groomed him. What a betrayal! He set the gun down on his lap, and she lowered her hands.

"What do you suggest?" he asked. "Blow up the rest home?"

"No," she said sadly. "But we are both being hunted. Sooner or later, they always get you. It's only a matter of time."

He nodded, then got up and slid the gun in the back of his pants.

"DePinko know I did it? The ball point pen tracheotomy?"

"Yeah. Cops are everywhere. He told them that he suspected you were bad news from the beginning."

"The joke is on him. I never signed his stupid evaluation," said Gabriel. "He can take his unsatisfactory and improvement plans and shove them up his ass."

Casey smiled.

"I think the best move is to go our separate ways. I'd love to head to Europe and spend some time painting in Southern France or something. I have like six passports."

"Six?" said Gabriel. "Try twelve for me."

He walked toward the door and looked back at Casey Cipriano one last time. He knew it was the last time he would ever see her. He opened the door and walked downstairs to his car out front.

When he got in, he thought about the Colonel and decided he should drive over to Broken Branches and kill him, instead. His flight wasn't until the morning, so he had time. It would be the best move for his future. When he turned the key of the Subaru, the engine stalled.

He knew he shouldn't try again, but he did anyway.

Casey heard the explosion from her bedroom and came to the window and studied the orange burning inferno outside. The Colonel's text had tipped her in to the Subaru Gabriel had just purchased and parked around the corner. She watched with a little sadness as Gabriel's car burned for a moment, then let the curtain slip back and picked up her passport and suitcase and moved toward the door.

She imagined herself sipping wine as she painted on the coast of Spain.

The only decision left for her to make was which passport she'd use this time.

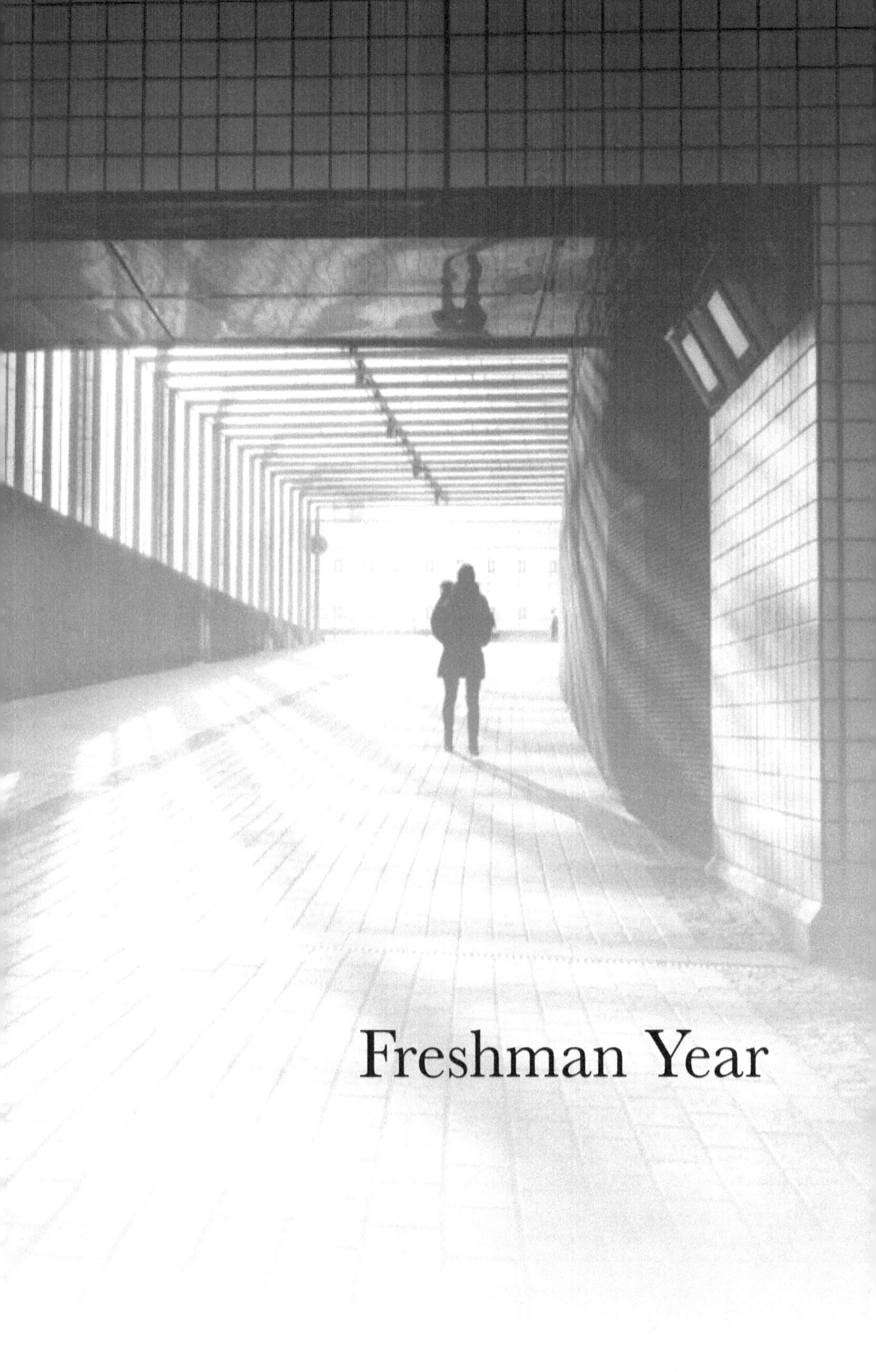
Freshman Year

I am standing on the corner of Commonwealth Avenue and Beacon studying the ivory snowbanks. Next to me is McAdams—of all people. He looks like a little kid, dressed in an oversized red parka with a winter hat; I'm in a black leather jacket.

For some reason, I start thinking about the symbolic nature of snow. I blame it on the fact that I had just finished reading *The Dead* by James Joyce a couple of nights ago. Joyce was always inferring that the snow meant winter more than just literal snow: death, darkness—the end of the line. And here I was with McAdams in his red parka, looking like the devil himself, literally standing at the end of the line. I look up as the B-Line rattles past us: the Green Line. We are at the farthest point that the tracks extend Boston to Chestnut Hill University.

The end of the line.

A wave of fatigue comes over me as I stand there with McAdams, waiting for the light to turn so we can cross. It's like I am paralyzed there, frozen in time, waiting to just disappear. The winter makes me think about hibernation—I've been so tired lately—all the miles, all the stress, all the expectations. The solar glare is making me squint, and a wave of sadness and bleakness overcomes me like it did for a disillusioned Gabriel Conroy, staring out at the snow falling all over the living and the dead in Ireland.

I feel completely hopeless.

This is literally the crossroads for me. The crossroads in life.

There was a surprise blizzard that struck Boston last night, one that postponed finals for the first time in university history, leading to the blur of events culminated with a "spontaneous blizzard party." I am positive it will take on a different name, as the days pass, when discoveries are made, and stories are told.

Then, there's also the fact that I can't locate my dad's cardinal red '79 Pontiac Bonneville. It's not in the location where I parked it last night. When McAdams and I went to the spot, it had been shoveled out with a beat-up kitchen chair.

I'm not even going to get into my failing grades after some disastrous semester exams.

My head throbs from the cheap beer I consumed last night, and it's worsened by McAdams high-pitched voice.

"I think someone may have shit in the closet last night," he suddenly states.

I look over at him, astounded, and laugh.

"What? Shit in whose closet?"

"Donnelly's.

Donnelly was a senior on the team who lived at 1880 Commonwealth Avenue, and always threw fun parties. He paid for everything because he was some sort of trust-funder or something. The shit in the closet was the thoughtless thanks for all his efforts. We were selfish, ungrateful pricks.

"You probably did it," I say. "You stink."

"Listen, Monty. I don't shit in the closets," he says defensively. "Maybe it was my brother, or his friend, Bill."

McAdams's brother had come home to Boston for Christmas. He was at UMass and Bill was his roommate. I wouldn't put it past them. I had heard that every college has some bizarre tradition, and at UMass it was probably shitting in the closet. It reminds me of the Dane Cook bit about shitting on the coats at a party, and then disappearing like a ghost. An Irish goodbye with a gift from a leprechaun. It is all disgusting—but this is college. People were mentally, ethically, and morally unsound, and throw in fallacious after twenty beers.

When the light changes from green to red, the crosswalk light turns white, and the clock starts counting down as we walk across Comm. Avenue slowly and begin to cover the mile back toward Chestnut Hill University's campus.

The delirium has faded—like I knew it would—and the hangover from last night sets in harder like the pressure I am feeling academically. I think about my failing, first semester grades, and it makes my head ache even more.

"You okay?" asks McAdams, as he sees me rubbing my temples.

"Nope. Twenty Black Labels will give you half of an aneurysm, especially at one-hundred-fifty pounds," I reply.

"The aim of the wise is not to secure pleasure, but to avoid pain," McAdams says. "Aristotle said that."

"Well, I wouldn't know since I am failing philosophy," I state defensively. "Delirium passes. James Joyce wrote that."

The upside is I am pulling an A in that *James Joyce* class, literally the name of the course, where we were assigned to read *The Dead*. The professor is an Irish Jesuit named Father James Michael Flynn. He was a Joycean scholar back in Dublin and now, at Chestnut Hill, they put in him charge of buying rare manuscripts like *Ulysses* and *Dubliners* first-editions. He liked me and I had spent time speaking with him during his office hours about James Joyce and Irish Literature—with "extended office hours" over at The Green Briar for a couple of Guinness.

"By the way, when is your meeting with the dean?" asks McAdams.

"Monday morning."

"Damn. Is she gonna cut you a break? I mean, freshman screw up the first semester all the time. You're not the first in history."

However, I have really screwed up this time by earning a 1.5 GPA. I failed theology, philosophy, and even after begging my adjunct professor, earned a D- in calculus. I bit off more than I could chew going to such a challenging academic school. Maybe a D2 or D3 school would have been a better fit.

"Wait a second," McAdams shouts. "Isn't that your father's car?"

I look up to see the cardinal red Pontiac speeding down the avenue.

Without hesitation, I begin to sprint as McAdams's hysterical laughter rises behind me. I trail the car at a clip of 4:30 mile and watch as it turns into a campus parking garage. I sprint up the ramp in hot pursuit and don't let up until I arrive at the driver's side window.

I've caught the thief. The hopeless feeling begins to fade for a moment and my adrenaline is surging.

"Hey! What the hell?" I shout, pounding on the window. "Why do you have my car?"

The steamy window powers down.

"Hey, Monty! What's up, bro?"

It's Logan, my blond-haired surfer teammate from California.

"Logan, why do you have my car?"

"You gave me the keys last night. You were really hammered and said, 'Logan, take these so I won't drive drunk.' Then you said some stuff about coming out with me to California for Christmas."

He gets out and tosses me the keys. It's a 1979 Pontiac, a ten-year-old, beat-up clunker, but my dad loves it for the velvet feel of the seats and the smooth ride. Honestly, I was damn lucky to get a car at school and breathe a sigh of relief at seeing a friendly face behind the wheel. Logan smiles.

"Let's go up to McCollin Commons and get some breakfast," he says.

Relieved, I lock the car and put the keys in my pocket, then begin walking with him.

"Dude, did you hear someone shit in the closet last night?" he asks.

***

There is one lap to go.

This is my last shot. If I hesitate, I could lose my chance to go to The Show.

The rumbling on the banked track in the Boston Memorial Armory becomes a vibration in my chest and legs. My lungs are on fire—partially due to the 2800 meters and the brutal pace at a 4:15 per mile—but also due to the cold and lingering pollutants that hang in the air of this ancient brick dungeon. Soldiers smoke cigars and cigarettes, while swilling Budweiser's, and placing bets on races from the balcony that encircles the arena above. Two kids from Penn are in front of me as I run in a pace line, trotting toward a personal best—and protential national qualifier.

I think about how I woke up this morning from strange dreams and went for a run at dawn. I jogged out onto the streets of Newton, then down into Brighton to shake out my legs before this race. Winter was here—rare piles of pure, ivory-colored but mostly dirty snow piled on the sidewalks between triple-deckers. I pulled my gray hood over my head like Rocky Balboa and jogged, a morning run, just to make sure my muscles were loose for the late morning race.

I am eighteen years and five months, and I am a freshman.

My metamorphosis from high school to college has been astounding. I knew I would end up in Boston for college. When a few races went my way during my senior year of high school, the phone started ringing with D1 coaches on the other end of the line. However, I never knew this athletic metamorphosis would bring me to the point where I would be punching my ticket to Indianapolis for the NCAA Championships. Four years ago, I was the slowest guy on the team. Cut to a year ago, I was at the top of the state. Now, I am on the verge of being among the top thirteen runners in the United States.

I edge up on the maroon and blue-striped Ivy League jerseys and plot my last 200 meters. I accelerate and drop the hammer, absolutely flying by them at full throttle speed. The cigar smoke from the drunk soldiers' seeps into my lungs, but I push through. The red digits are clicking in front of me like a bomb counting down to implosion. 7:57, 7:58...

I close my eyes and lean into the abyss.

***

When I open my eyes, I see the dean sitting in front of me reviewing my first semester transcript.

She is of Korean descent—I finally decide—with salt-and-pepper hair pulled back firmly in a bun. She wears a navy-blue Talbot's jacket, and a permanent frown on her aging face. In contrast, I spent fifteen minutes in the mirror staring at my pale face that is freshly shaved, sharp blue blazer, a white pressed shirt, a school tie with maroon and gold colors, caches, and brown penny loafer shoes that my dad shined for me the previous evening. The dean finally takes off her glasses and sets them down on my transcript and lets out a brief sigh.

"Montgomery, I'm going to be straightforward with you," she says. "Exactly how did you get into this university?"

I pause for a moment and ponder her question

"Ummm...I ran a mile," I say softly.

"You ran a mile?" she repeats in a questioning tone.

"What on earth does that have to do with anything? This is an academic institution. We are one of the finest in the Northeast."

"I was put on a short list. By my coach," I say softly, embarrassed by the words.

"Short list? Let me guess: Coach Randall? Jesus," responds angrily. "This isn't the damn Oscars. This is an esteemed university."

"Well, he recruited me, and I went on a list for admission. Guaranteed."

"We don't have 'lists' at Chestnut Hill, and there are no guarantees in life," she stammers, making the quotation marks with her fingers. "Do you even want to be here, Montgomery? As a student, that is."

I think about it. Do I even want to be here? Great question. The fact is that I love running, but in all honestly, between my hundred miles a week, and the fact I let my girlfriend select my courses last summer, I'm uncertain how to respond. Gina. She is an honor student at Amherst, and she picked a hard course load because I was too distracted by the delirium of love. I was clueless, caught up in my summer of love and training. But, as I sit here now, I realize that the delirium has most definitely faded. I am sober. When I arrived, the team doctor told me that I had mononucleosis, then I blamed her for destroying my cross-country season by giving me the virus. So, my immature response was to break up with her after a meet at Franklin Park.

However, it was more than that...she liked me too much. She was beautiful. Italian with a firm, bronzed body, and infectious smile. However, I realize as I sit here that I am selfish and incapable of appreciating love, but more importantly, I recognize my own good fortune because of the constant rejection and failure I experienced in my youth.

"Yes," I hear myself blurt. "I want to be here."

The dean frowns.

"Tell me why," she says. "What academic goals do you have?"

"You can see my strength is in the humanities... history and English. I can write," I blurt without hesitation.

The dean folds her arms pessimistically.

"Humanities? Well, what do you write? Give me some examples, Montgomery," she asks in an almost forgiving tone.

"Fiction."

"Well, you are certainly residing in a fictional world right now," she says firmly. "What else?"

"Lyrics, poetry… oh…and I have an internship with *The Boston Globe* next year," I tell her.

"Doing what?"

"School sports—Independent League—prep school football, track and field, and cross-country," I say with an air of pride in my voice. "I'll be published in the Sunday *Globe* weekly."

"Is this through our journalism program?"

"No. My high school journalism teacher is an alumnus and directed me to the internship since I had written for the local paper."

"What's his name?"

"John Sheehan."

She smiles.

"John was your teacher? He was my boy… well, a friend… back when we went to school here together," she says with an uncontrollable glee. "Tell him I said… hello."

And it occurs to me that I have discovered my dean's old love. The heart wants what the heart wants. She takes out her silver pen and writes down something on the paper in front of her and hands it to me.

"I'm giving you one semester," she says. "And I'm assigning you academic tutoring in theology and philosophy. Looks like the D- in calculus might just satisfy the math requirement."

She signs some more on the paper, then looks at me firmly.

"Monty, I'm giving you one semester to fix this, or you can take your running to another less-competitive university."

I beam and stand up and extend my hand. She rolls her eyes and shakes it.

"Thank you, Dean," I say. "I won't let you down."

***

It's the day after "The Mad Shitter's Day Party" as it has now been named. I am standing alone in a cooler in a liquor store in New Hampshire, wondering how I got here. Suddenly, I notice the lights are turning off. I remember my promise to the dean, and suddenly have a bad feeling, one of tremendous guilt and shame as if I were in the Garden of Eden and God was casting me into darkness. McAdams comes around the corner with two cases of Keystone Light with a devilish grin. He's still wearing that damn red parka.

"Hey, who turned the lights off?" he asks.

I push open the door of the cooler and watch the elderly owner lock the door and walk away.

"Wait!" we both scream.

I sprint to the door to see the old guy drive away.

"Shit! We're locked in!" I scream as McAdams comes up next to me.

"Yep. We are locked in a liquor store in New Hampshire during exams. And your point is?"

I look at him and shake my head.

"We have to get back. I have to study. Everything is on the line for me here, McAdams."

He laughs and cracks another beer.

"Come on, Monty. Drink up. This is a dream come true!"

"More like a nightmare," I say.

I wake up in the morning, on a bed of Budweiser cases, to the owner keying the door. I stand up and rub my eyes and look at my watch. It's 9 AM.

"Shit, McAdams. I have to get back. I have a tutoring session. The dean checks on my attendance."

The owner looks at me, then McAdams, who is terribly hungover.

"What the hell is this?" he shouts.

"You did this. We were in the cooler, and you shut the lights off and locked us in," I plead.

"I'm calling the cops!" he shouts.

I take out forty dollars in cash and set it on the counter.

"Sir, we didn't steal anything. Please."

He doesn't listen, picks up the phone and dials.

"Let's go, Monty!" McAdams shouts.

I am torn. I need to clear my name, but the owner is irate. I begrudgingly decide to follow my teammate.

McAdams gets in the Pontiac on the passenger side.

"Let's go. Punch it," he shouts, as if he is the devil himself.

The idea is insane. I drive but I have this sinking feeling. All this for a couple of cases of beer on a Sunday. Sure enough, as we approach the Massachusetts border, I see the cherry-top sirens light up behind me.

"Fuck, McAdams."

"Just keep driving. Get over the line, they can't arrest you if you are in another state," he commands.

I know his words aren't true, but my foot seems to agree with my rebellious friend. The cruiser is on our tail, and I see the borderline in front of me.

"Punch it, Monty!"

I take my foot off the accelerator and hit the brakes, pulling over slowly.

"What the hell? We're both going to be arrested now!" screams McAdams.

I rest my head on the steering wheel and think about escaping it all.

***

I call my cousin, Frank Bradley, who is a defense attorney down in Taunton, when I'm given my one phone call. He's worked some big cases, so I know he can bail me out of this one. He had given me his business card at my graduation party. Little did I know how soon I'd need to use it.

"New Hampshire?" he asks. "Do your parents know you're up there?"

"No. We were just getting some beer on a Sunday. Liquor laws, you know?" I tell him.

"Damn those Puritan Blue Laws. Okay. I know an attorney up there. Let me make a call, but Monty, I'm only doing this once for you," he says. "No more bailouts."

"Got it."

By noon, I am released. McAdams must wait for his father to come up and bail him out and curses me out when he hears I am in the clear.

I drive back alone down 128 to school and listen to a song on the radio about seeking shelter. I get back to my dorm and sleep for a few hours then go down to lunch and to my tutoring appointment like nothing had happened.

***

It's a few days later and the team moves as a pack up Heartbreak Hill, and McAdams moves to the front then the back, but as we begin to descend back toward campus, I notice that he slows and drops his pants, squatting down low.

"I knew it. He's the Mad Shitter!" someone screams as he defecates on the grass.

Donnelly's ears perk up and his face turns red. McAdams pulls up his shorts and bolts past us back to campus.

***

Randall comes out of the shower with just a towel and studies the track team, lying on the floor and lounging in chairs around the locker room after the long workout.

"National list is out," he shouts. "I have the list right here. Just came across on the fax machine."

He pulls it out of the top of his locker and holds it up.

I pick myself off up the floor. The Firehouse 10-miler at 5:30 pace has wiped me out, but I am up and alert now. Randall tapes the list to the wall and people crowd in around. I can't see.

"Did I make it, Coach?" I ask.

"You sure did, Monty," he beams. "First heat of the 3000 meters. You are going to The Show!"

I breathe a sigh of relief.

"Seems you made a good impression with the dean. She's giving you an academic waiver to complete," he says, handing me the paper.

The team is excited around me. I've done it. I am going to Indianapolis. Randall grabs me by the arm.

"But don't fuck up again, Monty," he whispers sternly. "Like getting locked in a liquor store in New Hampshire with that asshole McAdams. The kid is evil. Do you see how he's leading you down the highway to Hell? Yeah, I know about that."

He lets go of my arm a little too aggressively, and I watch in horror as Randall's towel falls to the ground. A stunned collective "ohhhhh" from the team comes.

Let's just say, that at fifty years old, he's lost his form from his Boston Marathon days.

***

Not to be histrionic or nostalgic about it all—but I remember vividly what happened out in Indianapolis. I tried my hardest and ran my best race; I have no regrets. The results cannot be changed.

"Just making it to Nationals, Randall told me after the race on the plane, "is the accomplishment of a lifetime."

That was thirty-two years ago: ancient history. My running days are over. I think back on the foolishness and ecstasy of my glorious freshman year—one where friendships were made, both good and bad—life-long friendships. McAdams died a year ago. It hit me hard when I attended his untimely funeral. My father always said that man has free will, and the devil didn't make you drink that alcohol—it was your choice. He was the son of an alcoholic who died at thirty-seven years old, so I never challenged his words.

I often think of verses that A.E. Houseman penned in "To an Athlete Dying Young." Most of that poem rings true about the short-lived glory of my college running career.

However, I'll always remember my freshman year.